THE WEIGHT OF PARADISE

THE

WEIGHT

OF PARADISE

IMAN HUMAYDAN

TRANSLATED BY MICHELLE HARTMAN

Interlink Books

An imprint of Interlink Publishing Group, Inc.
Northampton, Massachusetts

First published 2016 by

Interlink Books
An imprint of Interlink Publishing Group, Inc.
46 Crosby Street, Northampton, MA 01060
www.interlinkbooks.com

Library of Congress Cataloging-in-Publication data available

ISBN-13: 978-1-56656-055-9

Printed in the United States of America

To request our complete 48-page catalog, please call us
toll free at 1-800-238-LINK,
visit our website at www.interlinkbooks.com, or write to
Interlink Publishing, 46 Crosby Street, Northampton, MA 01060

I

BEIRUT, AUGUST 1978

Although her legs buckled under her and she almost fell onto the sidewalk, Noura kept walking, hurried and anxious. Her heart beat in her chest like a drum, living and screaming in her ears. She could no longer hear anything, except these terrified palpitations mixed with her increasingly tense panting. She no longer heard anyone, not even the voice of the man who'd started chasing her when she'd left the embassy after being told by a staff member to come back the following day.

Cars passed by at an insane speed, the burning sun reflecting off their hot, metal frames, making the city even hotter, as if hell had swallowed up the light of day and everything living within it. Distant gunfire drew closer and then farther away again, a swing set of sound. Its repeated rhythms drew lines in space. Artillery rounds, military jeeps, sirens. Noura hesitated between waiting it out somewhere nearby and hurrying home. But she thought waiting wouldn't work, there was no set time for the beginning or end of the violence—its ripples form, expand, and then end. People had become skilled at managing their lives in its shadow.

She could probably find a taxi to take her to the house of the woman who was looking after her child. Noura wasn't far from the embassy when this man suddenly surprised her by driving his car right alongside her. She thought he might stop and come after her, but instead it seemed as if he simply enjoyed scaring her.

She slowed down a little. "Where do you think you're going? I'm gonna follow you even if you go to outer space, you little spy," he said to her, leaning his head out the car window near the sidewalk she was standing on. "I'm gonna throw you to the dogs, you whore." She almost smiled, though she was afraid. She wanted to tell him that she would write and keep on writing, that she was married and had a child, that he—despite his job in the mukhabarat—didn't know that. She would survive. She could protect herself from him; this time he wouldn't be able to get to her. She kept on walking toward the main road, where she could find a taxi.

Noura thought about all the places she'd left behind since she'd quit Syria. During long walks through dewy spring grass, walks she used to take in the vineyards in the village of Rummaneh in the Jabal al-Arab, she used to think about trips she once took from Damascus with her university classmates, who, she'd heard, had been arrested two years ago; her ex-lover Suhayl, who visited her in Beirut and whom she'd helped to flee and get political refugee status in Sweden; her friends who were forced to migrate, escaping death; her father, who left prison only half a man; and her grandmother, whose voice kept her company even though she'd passed away years before. In her head, Noura went back to the time when she'd first arrived in Beirut and the years that had passed since then, the holidays she used to spend in her grandmother's village.

She thought about her sister Henaa, who killed herself there in the summer. The family covered up the suicide. They started spreading a story that she'd died of a bite from a poisonous snake hidden in the bakeh where they found her body. The bakeh was that room where they kept all the gardening supplies and pesticides, and where the animals sheltered during the winter. Noura knew the truth, though. She knew how her sister had died. She'd found her long suicide note in their bed at the house of their grandmother, Shehla, or Shahani, as she liked to be called. Noura read the letter and hid it deep in her underwear drawer. When she came back from the cemetery after her sister's burial she felt as if she were suffocating and wanted to scream but she had to stay silent, as if the reason for her sister's suicide were a disgrace to hide. A relationship with an army officer had resulted in a pregnancy. He told her to get rid of it. "It's your responsibility—get rid of it," he said, and then left. He stopped returning her calls. Instead she got rid of her own life. The night before Henaa killed herself, she woke Noura up by secretly sobbing next to her. They were sharing a bed and Henaa told her that she was suffering from menstrual cramps. Noura believed her. They hugged and then Noura went back to sleep, her hand remaining suspended on her sister's belly, the place she thought was the location of her pain, the very place that pushed her sister to commit suicide the next day.

oura remembered all of this as she threw herself into u.. taxi, looking at him sitting in his car parked on the side of the road through the window. When she turned her head around, he started his car and followed her.

"You don't deserve to live!" She thought about these words, which he repeated over and over again. She felt an anger so sweeping that—if she could harness its power—she would have been able to destroy the seat she was sitting on or kill that man behind her. Moments like these took her back to a reality she thought she'd moved beyond, to a past she imagined she'd finished with and left behind. But, no, now she was faced with a bolted door. She couldn't escape.

She got out of the taxi and rushed into a narrow alley off the Corniche al-Mezraa. She didn't want the driver to take her to her house, since she didn't want the person following her to know where she lived. She went into a little grocery store and disappeared for a few minutes. She wanted to call Sabah to make sure she'd gone to her apartment as Noura had asked her to do that morning, to take all of her things, including her child's clothes and his food. Noura wanted to tell her that she was afraid, that she wouldn't go back to her own apartment, because the person chasing her might have already investigated her and figured out where she lived. The telephone rang repeatedly and no one answered. She hung up and then left, telling herself that as soon as she'd escaped the man, she'd take another taxi. But suddenly she slowed her pace, as she thought back to the first moments of the day, when her son opened his eyes while Sabah was holding him in her arms. He looked at her for a second, and then smiled for the first time in his life that day, only to fall back asleep.

A weight was holding Noura down and preventing her from walking. She thought she was paying the price for a past that kept coming back to her, with which she had never settled her account. But she couldn't keep living always on the run. She had to stop a little to contemplate what she was doing. She'd become a mother now, her son's future was tied to her past in some way, and she didn't want to pass a hurtful past on to him. She would stop moving, she thought, she would turn around toward the car that was slowly following her, she would look the driver straight in the eye and tell him that she wouldn't stop at publishing her story about Henaa, but she would write about him once, twice, and a third time. She would publish what she wrote about the prisons where friends had disappeared into dark dungeons, about those people who had been her university classmates in Damascus, people who were missing, whose families didn't dare ask about them.

Perhaps Noura had stopped walking, perhaps she'd said a word or two. Perhaps she hadn't finished thinking about her last words. Perhaps her eyes hadn't looked straight into his eyes. Perhaps she hadn't completely turned around. Perhaps she'd thought that what was happening was a nightmare and she would wake up from it soon, or that an earthquake had left her paralyzed and speechless....

All of this happened in only a second.

Noura wanted to tell Henaa, whose life had ended through subjugation, that she'd published her story and that she, Henaa, had now been vindicated. She wanted to tell her that they killed her twice because they kept silent and indeed they were complicit, even though they knew the truth. Noura wanted to tell their late grandmother, Shahani, that she wouldn't forget her legacy, that she had a right to life. She wanted to tell. But she didn't tell. She couldn't. She couldn't after this day.

From the car window, a silenced bullet finished her off. It entered her neck, throwing her to the ground and silencing her. The envelope she was carrying flew up and all the papers inside it fluttered out and rose up in the air, the hot breeze playing with them, then scattering them all over the narrow sidewalk. One was a photograph of a baby.

The army officer got out of the car and stood looking at her lying on the ground. He walked over, lifted her by the arms, and then dragged her toward the car, pulling her body up and pushing it inside. He sat her in the backseat, propping up her head to lean it against the locked door. She was warm. Her eyes were open, looking at his face and blinking slowly. He raised her hand and started trying to take her twisted, snake-shaped gold ring off her finger. She felt pain diffusing through her limbs as she tried weakly to collapse her fingers inside her hand. She didn't want to lose this particular ring. She closed her eyes and saw that spring day when she was stretched out on the damp sand at the seashore. The sky was blue and she dozed off while the spray of the waves touched her hair and neck. The murderer pressed her cold hand to her chest as if he were throwing it far away from himself. A soft moan escaped her as he stuffed the ring into his shirt pocket.

The street was desolate, or this is how it seemed to her; no one came near them. Silence and fear ruled Beirut. A Syrian army officer was humiliating it, just as Israeli soldiers would humiliate it, just as the Lebanese militias would humiliate it in the future, again and again.

He drove the car slowly onto a street branching off onto the campus of Beirut Arab University, and parked on the side of the road by a little restaurant frequented by workers and taxi drivers. He got out of the car after taking his gun and other personal possessions. And he left.

**

A booby-trapped car exploded in the Fakhani area of Beirut. Fires and clouds of smoke. A long line of cars parked next to the burning building also caught fire. The glass of one of the cars parked at the top of the narrow road shattered, dust and stones raining down upon it. The body of a dead woman was stretched out on the back seat, blood covering her neck and soaking her blue cotton shirt, her head drooping over the seat and tiny pieces of shattered glass embedded in her hair and body.

A television report gave the location of the explosion and the names of most of the victims, and noted that an unidentified woman in her early thirties had been killed inside a car by shrapnel from the explosion.

There the report ended.

No one knew how that woman came to be in that stolen Peugeot with no license plates. No one knew that she'd come to Beirut to find freedom. No one knew that the deafening silence, which she had wanted to break, was what led to her death.

2
JUNE 1994

"Where are you going, Madame?" the taxi driver asked loudly, stopping his car near her and lifting her out of her thoughts, which had nailed her to the sidewalk she'd been standing on, unsure where to go.

Two months had passed since Maya arrived in Beirut from Paris. Many things happened in those two months. She saw her husband slowly die of cancer and then buried in his southern village, according to his wishes. She was alone now with their son, Shadi, and she had to accept this reality. It felt as if more than a year had passed since she'd been here.

"Ashrafiyeh?" Maya replied in the form of a question whose answer she already knew. The driver took off, lifting his chin up with obvious annoyance, meaning he refused to take her. A distance of less than five kilometers separated Hamra Street in West Beirut and Ashrafiyeh in East Beirut, but service taxi drivers usually refused to take her across, preferring passengers headed to the southern side of Beirut, which was much further away. They chose to go to there despite the distance and the traffic there. Although all signs of it have been removed since the war ended, the demarcation line between the two Beiruts remains firmly rooted in people's minds.

The loss of Zeyad was still fresh. They had come to Lebanon with Shadi, and Zeyad died in a hospital two weeks later. Maya hadn't known how to manage her life, and her son's life, since she learned of Zeyad's illness. It was as if death had come between them, and now they had nothing to do but wait. With the illness, her three-person family had increased in number. The illness was like an annoying, ever-present guest who must always be taken into account, a guest we can only dream of getting rid of. When we become aware that this guest will stay longer than expected, we start behaving differently.

In the beginning, Maya started moving as if on auto pilot: cooking automatically, dropping Shadi off at daycare, going with Zeyad to his chemotherapy treatments, then going back and starting her day's work. At the time she was working at home as a researcher and assistant to a French director who was making a documentary film about Arab cities. Often she would stand in the middle of the kitchen for minutes at a time staring out its tiny window into the emptiness. Feeling like a complete failure, she lifted her eyes, which collided with the tall gray buildings on the other side of the street. A kind of paralysis briefly prevented her from going out food shopping.

Finally, she flagged down a shared taxi. The driver fidgeted when Maya opened the front door of the car to sit there. A woman sitting in the front seat might mean losing his fifth passenger if all three back seats filled. Many men would be embarrassed and hesitate to sit next to a woman in the front seat. He pulled away angrily before she'd even shut the car door, her body still hanging outside. "Ya Allah," she heard herself saying, and wanted to admonish the driver for his aggressive behavior. However, one glance at his scowling face led her to reconsider. He was a powder keg about to explode. This all happened in a flash, without the driver paying attention or saying even one word to apologize. She thought that talking was sometimes useless and that in a fraught and anxious atmosphere—like Beirut's, emerging from the long tunnel of the war—silence was the ideal solution for its economy of nerves.

However, the economy of nerves that Maya chose didn't yield anything, since the car's motor died suddenly in the middle of the bridge leading to Sodeco Square. The driver got out and started swearing, lifting the hood. Then he sat back down and tried several times to make the motor turn over, to no avail.

"Damn this day!" he shouted, "A disaster from the start. What brought me here?" He then got out of the car and started inspecting the motor again, trying to get it running. After a few minutes, he approached, opened the car door on Maya's side and told her, in an uncompromising, critical tone: "Get out here, sister, find your own way, here's the 1,000 lira you already paid."

Maya had already been thinking that something like this would happen before she got to her friend Sarah's café. Therefore when she heard what the taxi driver said, she didn't object. Indeed her body, which had been on high alert, started to relax, and moved toward the door automatically, as if already prepared. She grabbed her handbag and left the money on the seat. She walked toward the crossing between Bechara El Khoury and Sodeco Streets, while observing the shapes of the scattered clouds spring had left behind in the June sky.

Nazar, the shoemaker in the Strand Building, had made no mistakes in Arabic when talking to her the day before: "Everything's up there … there in your head … in your head. Beirut is still divided up there…. there." His right index finger was pointing at his temple. She had come to pick up her old shoes, which he'd repaired and shined. "New, just like they used to be," as he liked to say, adding in his charming Armenian accent, "Beirut isn't divided only into two. Beirut's a hundred parts … and you land where chance puts you."

"Up there, in your head, up there," Nazar always told her, not just to describe Beirut but also when he talked about Yerevan, the capital of Armenia. He'd recently visited Armenia, the country of his ancestors, and he'd returned to Beirut with a huge feeling of loss. He'd dreamed about it for sixty years, almost the amount of time he'd spent in Beirut. One visit there was enough to know he'd lost it forever.

The Yerevan he dreamed of was "up there, in his head," he told Maya in a broken voice, disappointment depriving him of both confidence and resilience.

Nazar had put on weight and gone totally bald. When Maya returned to Lebanon, he reported to her that he'd lost his mother two years before. He had been living with her in an apartment near the Mayflower hotel, not far from where he worked. He was alone now. Maya remembered the first time she'd gone into the Strand Building searching for his shop. Sarah had recommended him to her. Maya asked the doorman on the ground floor about him. "Nazar the Armenian?" he answered with a question. No one knew Nazar's family name; it was enough just to say "the Armenian" to indicate whom you meant. The Armenians had been Lebanese for more than eighty years. However, this fact changes nothing for those in Lebanon who live behind the walls of their own communities, not interacting with people outside them.

Before she traveled abroad, Maya always used to visit Nazar, who sat in a wooden chair covered in red leather that he'd upholstered himself. She looked at him while he worked behind his shoe-sewing machine or near the small table, which was covered with every type of dye. He'd order coffee for her and invite her to stay a bit longer. It only took one little question for him to start talking and not stop. She knew she had a bad memory, so she found herself sometimes noting down a short sentence or two of what he'd said. Today he gave her an old issue of a Lebanese magazine published in French, devoted to Armenia. He told her that he'd saved it for her to read, then asked her to come back in two hours to pick up her shoes.

Maya always brought her old shoes that needed repairing to Nazar. She would throw them away only when Nazar had decided that they would be too difficult to repair. She believed that a special relationship develops between shoes and their owners—different than that between people and other objects in their immediate surroundings. Words her friend Bruno, the French director, had once spoken to her on this subject still rang in her ears: one day she'd arrived at his office running and gasping for air, her shoes damp from the rain and snow. He described how a shoe could take the shape of its owner's foot and carry its history, though shoes keep their own memory, independent of the memory of others, since they live their own experiences and see the world from a different perspective.

She went down the Strand Building's staircase out onto Hamra Street; she walked toward Café Wimpy. It was a pleasant day though spring had already ended. This street had changed since she'd left Beirut. It had been dying for years, and began now to recover a part of a former life, something of its glow, after it had transformed in the war into a den of spies, mukhabarat, detention centers for abducted civilians, and offices for local militias who became established thieves.

Maya felt exuberant that life was regaining its old pulse, even if slowly. While she was crossing the street and looking in the windows of new shops with international names, she saw renovation and reconstruction sites throughout the neighborhood. She didn't know at that moment that peace would destroy the café she was heading toward, which had survived the war years but would close to transform into a big ready-to-wear apparel chain. The shop windows displayed an attractive elegance, but an overflowing memory of loss lurked behind them. Beirut, she mused, was a giant repair shop not only for shoes and buildings. People also went out onto its streets with new faces and bodies. Despite its fabricated youth reshaped by scalpels, faces carried the memory of a former pain that was difficult to erase. Beirut was a city of metamorphosis. This was not just a real metamorphosis, but also a symbolic one. For some reason, the new face a person went out onto the streets with carried the violence of the past and its rejected memories. It was as if by denying them, they become stronger and more vivid, and violence would find its way out, becoming more ferocious.

Her body's reflection appeared on the glass in front of the clothes, like the presence of a friend she hadn't seen in a long time. How much time had passed since a man had touched her body? Maya carried on to the café, feeling her face, her fingers passing over it as if she wanted to be sure that it had not changed yet, that it was still the mirror of her soul. But how could she know that her face was still as it had been before and that she was still able to know the woman she had been?

She went into Café Wimpy and ordered a cup of coffee and a pack of Gitanes Lights, after sitting down near the window. It was still too early for Danny to have arrived. He was her old classmate from her university days in Beirut, and she was going to work with him now shooting a film on the reconstruction of downtown Beirut. She took a notebook out of her purse in which she had started writing down the broad strokes of the film's screenplay. In the first part of the notebook were bits of research she had done about the life of Asmahan. She knew she should leave aside all writing and work full time on completing the film first. But every time she tried to write, she found herself writing about her own life, about Zeyad's rejection of her as a woman after she'd gotten pregnant with her son Shadi. Now she was writing about his passing and a death inside herself that she had resisted since her return. She thought that she wouldn't be able to write a film script about the reconstruction of buildings, that she wouldn't be able to do this kind of work at all, while feeling so confused. Perhaps she should tell Danny when he arrived.

She felt a brunt of guilt that weighed on her more heavily than the loss of Zeyad. How could she live her life if she was unable to come to terms with his death? It had been six weeks since his passing. Her heart was heavy with something hazy, full of loss. She was thinking about her past and present life, about the drought of nearly four years that she'd lived without a sensual touch from the man who shared her bed. She was thinking about the many words that remained suspended in her throat and that she couldn't say. She was thinking about all that and what she would do tomorrow, the next day, and the one after that.

"It's hard to think about the future and connect to life if we don't first know how to live with loss," she wrote.

The two of them decided to return from France to Lebanon because Zeyad wanted to die in his village. He wanted to be buried next to his mother. It was the first time he'd insisted on a decision and not gone back on it. Maya didn't object to Zeyad's decision to return. At first he didn't believe how life threatening his illness was. He told her that he would get better soon, but he was fading away every day. Later, after undergoing many painful chemotherapy sessions with no result, he surrendered. She had never in her life felt so weak as she did after the doctor announced the results of the tests to them. "He might live a year, or perhaps a little bit less. That's all I can say," the doctor announced simply without any preliminaries. Neither she nor Zeyad was prepared to hear this truth. They were busy arranging their separation, each of them blaming the other for the failure of their relationship. Their happiness hadn't lasted for more than the seven years before she got pregnant. The birth of Shadi was the most important event in her life—not only because she became a mother but also because Zeyad became another man, and not at all like the man whom she'd met nine years before.

He postponed the discussion about her desire to have a child every time she brought it up. She would grow silent and lose her enthusiasm, after she heard him say, "We'll talk later." She started reading about how getting pregnant when you are older could be detrimental to the child, as well as being afraid that she would lose the desire to bear children and be a mother if Zeyad continued to refuse to consider it. Now she wondered about why she hadn't really deeply questioned the motives for his refusal, but only listened to the same arguments repeated again and again—like saying that their flat only had a living room and one bedroom and it was very small for three people, or that what he earned wasn't enough to pay for a child's needs.

The mere thought that Zeyad's family might someday take her son away terrified her. She knew that she had no relationship with them, and in the beginning she didn't care. But, now, after Zeyad's death, she had to deal with them directly, with no middleman, since she was scared of losing

Shadi. Islamic law states that upon the father's death, the right of custody for a male child goes to his paternal uncle or grandfather at the age of seven. In this were to be the case, Shadi would only be with her until he turned seven and then they would take him. This alone could push her to return to France. For sure, Maya would implement the decision well before Shadi turned seven, and definitely more quickly than she had her first decision to go abroad: she had thought about immigrating for years before finally packing her bags and getting herself to the airport. It took Maya a long time to make decisions. Her mother, Aida, confirmed that this trait was a part of her personality. She said that her daughter's slowness was something that dated from the time she was still in the womb. She'd hesitated a long time before coming into the light of a world that, by the time she crossed the threshold into adolescence, had transformed into darkness by a never-ending war.

Maya's life in France seemed like a dream. Ten years passed like it wasn't real. It became a reality only after the birth of her son. She spent seven days in the birthing clinic in Paris and another week at home waiting for her mother to arrive because she'd had a delay in getting her visa at the French embassy in Beirut. She was counting the days, actually the hours. She had no idea how to take care of a baby. She filled one whole bookshelf with books on how to take care of a newborn though her reading didn't give her self-confidence. She had never been interested in books about children. Her main interest was acquiring antique books, which had been removed from or forgotten in libraries and bookshops. She searched for them at the Avicenne bookshop in Paris, at the flea market, and in countless other places. She was the youngest in her family of three children—a boy and two girls. There had never been another baby in her family; she had never taken care of a baby. When she came back from the hospital to her little apartment with her newborn, Maya cleaned him with moist wipes and scented baby lotions. Her baby had not seen water since he left her womb. She was afraid to put him into the little bathtub. She thought he might get sick, for example, or that the humidity might get into his lungs and he wouldn't recover. When Aida came from Beirut, the first thing she did was take off Shadi's clothes, pour warm water over him and let him kick his legs around in the water happily. He let out sounds, periodic gasps of breath, his hands drawing circles in the air.

Maya sat on a low chair near Aida, who was using liquid soap on Shadi's body while intoning tenderly, "How can a child raise a child!?" "I'm not a child, Mama," Maya interrupted her in protest. "Don't forget I am thirty-seven years old. Women my age in the village in Lebanon are waiting to become grandmothers."

But Aida paid no attention to such words, since in her mind, her children would never grow up even if they reached their thirties and became parents themselves. She was happy that her daughter let her look after Shadi for a whole month, the entire time she was at her place in Paris. This was enough time for her to put behind her the disappointment she'd felt when her son Nadim's first daughter was born. Aida had traveled to Montreal believing that her son's Canadian wife would be happy she was there to care for her newborn. But the young woman forbade her to touch the baby. She was afraid that her infant daughter would pick up "germs" her grandmother might have carried in her breath from Lebanon, which was living through war and was afflicted by a lack of basic life requirements like health services.

Maya was happy that Aida was there, despite all the changes she had to make so the tiny apartment would be big enough not only for her new baby but her mother too. She put her in the only bedroom so she could sleep on the double bed near the baby's cot. She moved to the living room with Zeyad to sleep on the big pull-out sofa they'd bought especially for the occasion, just before Aida arrived. This arrangement wasn't practical for Maya while she was breastfeeding Shadi at night, but it didn't bother her. In fact, she was inundated by deep feelings of trust, knowing that her son was in safe hands.

While her mother was there, the tiny Parisian apartment transformed into a house ringing with laughter, the songs of Asmahan and Fairouz warbling through its small space, making it seem more expansive and welcoming, and the aroma of the oriental spices and flavors Aida had brought from Beirut wafting out of the kitchen. When Aida met some of the Arab neighbors who lived on their street, Maya was amazed at how quickly her mother got to know people and invited them over for coffee and meghli, the spiced rice pudding prepared when a baby is born. When Zeyad got back from work, he would find his living room filled with guests he'd never seen before except waiting for the elevator or on the roads nearby their building, at 10 Rue Jeanne d'Arc. He greeted them from the living room door without coming in, then silently withdrew to the bedroom, whose door was locked so that their voices wouldn't wake Shadi. Then he would go into the kitchen, the only empty place, to drink tea. At that time, Zeyad seemed like a stranger amid people who were there for the occasion of birth of a baby, the idea of whose conception he had rejected for so many years. He was proud of himself for receiving a positive reply to his request to increase the number of hours he was teaching Arabic language classes at one of the universities. He did this to supplement his salary, but he hadn't found the opportunity to inform Maya about it, taken as she was by her new motherhood.

3
JULY 1994

Maya stopped her car on the side of the Corniche al-Manara by the sea. Shadi got out angrily, as if being forced. She was on the verge of losing her patience with him: he didn't want to walk, didn't want to be next to her, and didn't want to listen to what she said. She stood near the iron fence, pointing at a faraway ship that seemed suspended on the horizon. She told him that the ship would keep waiting there until the sea calms down. She continued on, saying that she too, like that ship, was going to wait for him to calm down and listen to her. A wave rose up and crashed into the green fence that had turned brown with rust. They stepped back a little so as not to get sprayed by the wave. About to cry, Shadi said in protest: "This sea is small; it's dirty too. I don't like this place—the water here is salty."

"But all seawater is salty," she interrupted.

He didn't answer, but let go of her hand suddenly and started running in the opposite direction of where they were walking, upset and screaming: "*Je n'aime pas ici, je veux retourner chez nous*—I don't like it here, I want to go back home." He stopped, turned toward her, looked at her angrily, and told her in a broken voice, that he didn't like her, either, his crying escalating. "I want Teta Aida!"

Shadi wanted to go back to stay with his grandmother. He refused to keep walking with his mother. Maya reflected a bit and decided to go back to the car and drop him off at home.

"We're going back!" she told him, in a serious tone, while she was buckling his seat belt over him in his car seat. This wasn't the first time Shadi had expressed anxiety and agitation. Maya understood this and also that children—even at a very young age—feel loss, deprivation, and the lack of love between their parents. Maya remembered what Zeyad told her in the Parisian hospital before they returned to Beirut despite his intense drowsiness after taking the painkiller the nurse had given him: "I don't understand why you're still here. It's you who asked for a divorce!"

She thought about what he was saying and didn't answer. He didn't understand that their separation no longer meant anything to her at this critical moment, given his health situation. He didn't understand that she was no longer angry with him. He didn't understand that she only wanted him to forgive her if she had caused him any harm and not to feel any guilt toward her, either. He didn't understand that she could disagree and separate from him when he still had a future. She could leave him mercilessly when he was totally healthy, not haunted by death. But how can we abandon someone who won't live to see tomorrow?

That night, Maya couldn't go home and leave him in the hospital. She stayed nailed to the plastic chair facing his bed. Only a few meters separated them—the space occupied by the hospital bed and the supplies around it. She was looking at him as if she had never seen him before: the shape of his eyes, the roundness of his face, the color of his hair. She looked at the equipment surrounding him and the clear plastic bag attached to his hand through which the treatment reached his veins. She realized that she hadn't ever looked at his hands in this much detail. She'd never paid attention to them before. They'd kept evading her in bed for years before Shadi was born. Despite this she'd never paid attention to how thin and delicate his fingers were, until he was supine in a hospital bed. *We spend years with someone and never pay attention to the shape of their hands except at the moment of separation,* thought Maya, while observing the medicine dripping down from the bag hanging above his head. Light shone on it, reflecting the undulating colors dominated by gray. The drops flowed down through a long rubber tube, connecting to his veins through a little needle stuck into the back of his hand, whose skin color had turned a brownish blue.

She changed the bag as the nurse taught her, but nonetheless she now still pushed the call button afterward. She wasn't sure how much liquid entered the veins of his left hand. She isn't sure it's enough. She isn't sure where the needle should be. She tells herself that she isn't experienced and wonders why she is being asked to do all this, when it's not her job. "I'm not a nurse," she once said in an audible voice, and all of a sudden she became aware that what she'd said might bother Zeyad.

Their gaze met silently, momentarily, and then parted.

4
THE PARIS YEARS

When she was still in France and first pregnant with Shadi, Maya woke up at dawn to find Zeyad had started making love with her when they were half asleep. Her dream was still stuck in her head: she collected old books that she'd found among huge piles of rubble and destruction. She repaired the ripped pages and tried to make them back into books. She collected baby clothes from the clothesline on the roof of her parent's mountain house in Lebanon, then when she was finished couldn't find the stairs to climb back down. She started telling him what she'd seen in her dream, while his penis demonstrated the waning of his desire. After a bit, he came close, kissed her head, and whispered to her that he would love her forever. She felt that he was making a big effort to say those words, as if to convince himself that his love for her wouldn't change despite her pregnancy or another emotion he had that she didn't know about. She felt all of this but didn't know how to express it.

"But we can't completely control our emotions," she told him, as if she were in a different place. He looked at her inquiringly and surprised by her answer. Her words scared him; perhaps they mirrored his own feelings that he didn't want to admit. No doubt she must have hurt him in one way or another, because he felt deep down that she meant *his* emotions and how they'd changed. There was a long silence between them. She interrupted it after a moment to say that she didn't know what pushed her to respond like that, and that she didn't feel good. She said, "Maybe my response was only a way to soothe my anxiety." *Tétine pour mon angoisse— The anxiety of the end of love*, she thought to herself.

He passed his fingers over her naked breasts, looking at her face. It seemed as if he were looking at emptiness. She turned her back trying to go back to sleep. She was wounded by something she couldn't express clearly and was on the verge of crying. It was the last time that they held each other when naked.

She was to remember that night well, since afterward he never came close to her again. Despite this, she maintained the illusion that everything was fine. As if she were saying that she was happy with what she was carrying inside her, and didn't feel the need to share that growing love with anyone. *Love is there*, Maya thought, *Zeyad whispered it in my ear many times while making love, when he was inside me and wouldn't pull out until I asked him to when I was half asleep. But after Shadi's birth I lost that singular feeling of joy.*

Zeyad distanced himself increasingly and started sleeping in the living room. As if that distance were like the slow erosion of the relationship, which had turned over time into a rusty memory. She took refuge in Bruno, their mutual French friend, in his apartment one night and started crying as she took off her clothes, asking him out loud, "Am I a woman? Am I missing something? What has made our lust turn to ashes every night? We've started to kill love every morning—did we have to kill it to assert its presence?" Bruno stood stunned in front of her nakedness and the oddness of the scene, while she continued asking questions, sobbing like a toddler, "Am I a woman or not? Answer me!"

Maya stood up to leave the Parisian hospital room to go out into the long corridor, believing that Zeyad had fallen asleep. A memory of the first time they met flashed through her mind—actually it was their first date. Bruno, the director who she was working with, was a friend of Zeyad's at the time and he initiated that first meeting. They wanted to see the film, *Under the Volcano*, set in Mexico. They met in front of the entrance to the cinema. He put his hand in his pocket and discovered that he had forgotten his wallet in the jeans he had changed out of before leaving. He was embarrassed and stressed out. At that moment she was in love with the fact he was so worried, that she could feel how vulnerable and fragile he was. She took some money out of her purse and paid the young woman sitting behind the ticket counter. This was an automatic reaction and Maya didn't understand why he had to apologize. Then they forgot about it and Zeyad calmed down. They left and went for a long walk through the Latin Quarter to the university area where Maya's room was. They talked about the film and Mexico, because Zeyad had gone there to meet his uncle who had emigrated and his cousins who were born there. They talked about the Day of the Dead, other Mexican holidays, and traumas that burrow into a person's spirit and change his or her life.

Zeyad used to have to be hospitalized for one night after each chemotherapy treatment. His body wasn't able to withstand the effects. He also had to take another treatment just to prevent nausea and vomiting. The skin on his hands and arms blackened and his face grew darker. Large circles ringed his eyes, draining away their radiance. When Maya hugged him she felt that she was searching for a past only a tiny trace of which remained.

She put on her coat and started wanting to go back home, but Shadi insisted on staying with Zeyad, who had become tense because of the argument between the two of them in the room. After Zeyad fell ill, Shadi had become aggressive and agitated. Once, before they returned to Lebanon, he told Maya, crying, "You don't love Baba."

She went out onto the tiny balcony of the hospital room, leaving Shadi to play with his toy cars on the bed near Zeyad. Drops of rain moistened the metal sides of the balcony. She let the raindrops fall on her hair and shoulders. Her warm tears rushed down her face while she inhaled cigarette smoke in the heavy evening air. Fog covered the space between the balcony and the large trees that filled the hospital garden. For years, she hadn't seen such warm temperatures in a sunless Parisian winter. She wiped her tears and thought for a moment about the tulip bulbs that she had planted at the end of October, and how she had seen their shoots that morning, growing toward the light in pots on the balcony of her little apartment. Spring still hadn't come yet, but nature had lost all reason and flowers started blooming in winter. She put out her cigarette and went back into the room. It was calm inside. Shadi didn't want to go home though it was seven in the evening. Sometimes she felt a total powerlessness far exceeding her capacity to overcome it. Drops flowed down through the tubes and entered Zeyad's veins, mixing with his blood. He had to rely on a liquid diet as nourishment, since he could no longer eat food.

She heard a ringing sound coming from inside her purse, and started searching for her mobile phone in the bottom of the bag but couldn't find it. The phone went quiet, and she breathed a sigh of relief. However, its silence lasted hardly one minute before the ringing started again. Who was this insisting on reaching her? She found the mobile, took it out, exasperated, and looked at the number. Her sister Nada was calling from Beirut. She went out onto the balcony again to not disturb Zeyad. She answered and said that she was in the hospital and that Zeyad was doing the same. She had to start back from the beginning with Nada, every time—to inform her about Zeyad's condition from zero.

"You too, kiss Mama for me," she ended the conversation, feeling suffocated. Every time Nada called her, confused feelings of disappointment and regret assaulted her; she didn't know how to deal with them.

Their relationship worsened during the fall of the previous year, when Nada visited Paris with her husband and Maya told her about wanting to get divorced. This all happened before Zeyad's diagnosis.

On one of those days, they met in a café and Nada surprised her by posing nonstop questions: "Does he hit you at all?" Taken aback by the question, Maya responded quickly, "No, of course not!" "Is he stingy with you?" She hesitated, then answered, "No."

"Does he smoke pot? Take drugs? Cheat on you? Is he a gambler?"

"That's not our story Nada. You don't get my situation."

As if she weren't listening at all to what Maya was saying, she continued her interrogation, lowering her voice as if she were telling a secret.

"He can't get it up? Or is it that he can, and he's asking you for things in bed that you won't do?"

Despite her anxiety and worry, Maya was surprised by this last question and masked her embarrassment with loud, unstoppable laughter. She hadn't expected Nada to bring up the issue of their sexual relationship and what they did in bed. They were sisters, true, but their age difference never allowed Maya to feel that they were really friends—not to mention that Maya lived abroad, far from home and the family. She kept laughing tensely and Nada was surprised. "Be honest with me, we're sisters."

Maya stopped laughing. She'd lost any desire to keep talking with Nada. She crossed her hands behind her head and looked up at the sky.

The sun was shining in the air over Paris; it felt like a historic day to Maya. A full month had passed since she had last seen the sun. She'd seen nothing but gloomy gray, a low sky heavy on her heart and eyes almost crashing into the roofs of the city's buildings. She wanted to recapture joy once again that day—even if only a little—like a puppy shaking off the cold and dampness to be warm again. But Nada's questions were stressful, since they made Maya feel like her head was under water. She lifted her face hoping that Nada would stop this chatter, which only increased her feelings of loneliness. It was inevitable that she would crash into a wall. Maya just had to face what was happening alone while her sister would keep throwing questions at her that made her feel as if the two of them weren't alike at all. The image she had of her sister when she left Beirut began to disintegrate and disappear—what she remembered about her had nothing at all to do with what she was seeing and hearing now.

"It's better to leave it there, enough!" Maya interrupted her sister. "Let's enjoy the sun, wouldn't that be better? I feel like you are interrogating me and putting the blame on me, as if I'm guilty. It's exactly what the cops do with a woman who complains about her husband beating her up. I'm not complaining. I am just deciding to get a divorce."

Nada couldn't believe what she was hearing so she kept asking questions, this time in a louder voice, "And then what? You are totally hiding something from me, I'm sure of it. Are you having an affair? Tell me! You killed yourself to get married to him.... Our uncle's family stopped speaking to our mom for four years because you married a man from outside our community. And now you just want to divorce him. At the very least, they'll all say, 'If you take a donkey up the minaret, you'll be the one to bring it back down again. Or, you made your own bed, now you have to lie in it.' No one in the family is going to stand by you, and ..."

Maya interrupted her again, sharply, as if Nada's implicit accusation of infidelity were forcing her to respond: "Zeyad doesn't love me anymore, and ..."

But she wasn't even able to finish her sentence without feeling suffocated. She stopped a bit and then continued, shaking her head: "How could you want me to stay with a man who won't touch me? He hasn't come near me in three years, from the time I was pregnant with Shadi. *Khalas!*"

Maya felt exhausted. She inhaled deeply, as if she had just suddenly escaped from an airless room. She looked at Nada's face and found her staring back at her, astonished and harsh.

"He doesn't love you anymore...? But he didn't ask for the divorce—you are asking for it. Why? What's your problem? Live like he's not there, as if he's dead. You say he doesn't love you; what does *love* have to do with marriage? What *is* marriage ... some kind of game?"

At that moment, Nada's voice faded. Maya could no longer hear either it or any other sound around them. *Thank the Lord I am able to block out wounding, violent words*, Maya said to herself.

A buffer wall shielded her ears from Nada's voice. Despite this, Nada's words somehow took Maya back to the beginning of her relationship with Zeyad. She could no longer remember the details of their first years together or even the years of the war in Lebanon before she came to France, where she met him. *Surely memory is as short-lived as a moment of happiness*, Maya thought. *We've lived lives full of mistakes inside and outside of the war, but life has flooded us with countless moments of happiness.*

"I'm going to return to Lebanon with Shadi after the divorce. Zeyad will stay here. We decided to divorce in Paris so I can have custody of Shadi. That's what we agreed."

"What?" Nada interjected, sarcastically. "So you two have also made decisions about Shadi? This means there's no point in us discussing the divorce with you. It seems it's a final decision! But how will you and your son live, tell me that? Have you thought about this at all? Our dad passed away and left us almost nothing. We spent everything that he had on hospital bills before he died. Surely you know the whole story, so there's no point repeating it. Our mother sold land to pay for your school fees and Nadim's too. And, as you know, her pension isn't enough for her to live on and I pay for her to have a maid in the house. Nadim contributes nothing. He left and hasn't looked back since he got married in Canada. Did you think about all these things before making your decision? Or are you relying on the 400,000 Lebanese lira that Islamic custody laws require Shadi's father to pay you in child support?"

Nada studied law but stopped practicing when she married a man twenty years her senior, and now she is lecturing me on fine points of family law, Maya thought to herself bitterly without answering.

There are moments when we no longer think like others. Calculations that seem crucial to other people become superficial and unimportant to us. Everything depends on what we feel, where we are in the human condition, and how much of the loss of this condition we are able to bear. Maya thought about all this and said tensely, on the verge of tears, "Nada, try to understand! I discovered that I don't know the man I've been living with for eight years. I don't understand him. Could you live with a man in such a situation?"

"What do you mean you don't *know* him?" Nada asked her, "Do you mean he's gay?"

"I don't know…. Maybe!" Maya shouted at her sister and followed up angrily, "If that's the answer that will make you happy, yes, OK, let's say he's gay."

Nada realized that Maya had started getting angry and that she was expressing her discomfort with the dark humor well known to everyone in their family. She looked at Maya's face for a quick second, picked up her handbag that was resting on the chair next to her, took some francs out, put them on the table, and said, "Do what you want." Then she left the café, taking leave of Maya with a slight nod of her head and almost no words.

**

Maya went back home from the Parisian hospital with Shadi. Before falling asleep that night, he told her that she was hurting him and squeezing his chest. He said this suddenly, without any lead-in, while she was holding him in her arms, sitting on his bed, telling him little stories, as she did every night. He continued, saying that he was tired and wanted to go to sleep. She removed her arms, kissed him, and got out of his bed. She turned out the light and went into the living room where she slept. She knew that Shadi was angry and also that the reasons for his anger were difficult and complicated. She knew he blamed her both for the problems that he had witnessed between his parents and also for his father's illness. She felt confused about this—she didn't know what to tell him or do for him. His anger silenced her. She was silent and grew soft and distant. Nousa, the kitten she'd found a few months earlier, was standing at the threshold of his room waiting for her. Nousa looked at her, lifting her head to show the lone white spot on her neck of shiny black fur that was like an oasis of light. She wanted to be picked up and have her soft fur stroked; in those moments Maya had similar desires. She wanted to lay her head on someone's shoulder, close her eyes, and fall asleep. Nousa gave one long, faint meow, like a woman's moan. Her meow was slow and wounded. *She is exhausted, too*, thought Maya, *exhausted by waiting, by the silence emitted by the vibrations of perpetual anxiety, by my absence from the little house all day long.*

**

Maya was finishing her first year of university in Paris when she met Zeyad; she had yet to acclimate to either her new surroundings or the university. She would never had thought that in Paris she would go back to her studies, after having finished a humanities degree in Beirut. One day she packed her suitcase and went to Paris with her friend Sarah, who then returned to Beirut fairly quickly. But Maya remained, starting another life in France. She met Zeyad for the first time in May 1985. He was writing his doctoral dissertation and teaching

Arabic classes. She would never forget the morning when Sarah called her from Beirut to inform her that the French researcher Michel Seurat had been kidnapped on the airport road. Sarah had met him when he was with Palestinian friends who worked with her. She said that no one knew his whereabouts yet. The Islamic Jihad group announced that it had kidnapped him. A long time would pass, during which many people disappeared, before international reports according to which most of the kidnappings of foreigners in Lebanon had been undertaken at the behest of the Syrian mukhabarat and carried out by local groups.

That day Maya had a lunch meeting with Bruno, the French director she worked for. At the time, she was doing research for him about Cairo during the first half of the twentieth century, about the city's theater and arts scenes in the era before Nasser came to power, and more broadly about its social and cultural life. This work led her to find books and articles about the life and death of the legend she loved: Asmahan.

Despite scattereded showers, the sun shone through the clouds that day as she headed for lunch, shyly heralding the warmth of spring. Maya looked out the window of the bus headed for Boulevard St. Germain at the rainbow that had appeared on the horizon for a few minutes, and then dissipated and disappeared behind the clouds, moving toward the middle of the sky. She kept thinking about getting off the bus and going back home. Her conversation with Sarah—who had become practically her only connection to what was happening in Beirut—made her feel sad. Maya imagined what state of mind Sarah was in now. This was not the first time one of them had lost someone in the war. Perhaps those they'd lost hadn't really been their friends, and perhaps the loss hadn't been devastating, but it was enough to know a person—to have once seen their eyes sparkling with life and hear their voice speaking about their dreams—to feel their absence, to feel you had lost a friend.

At that moment, Maya felt no desire to see anyone. She wanted to go back to her room and call her mother. Maya hadn't phoned her in more than two weeks. She usually rang her from a phone booth not too far from the university residence hall where she lived. She'd learned how to use public phones without spending huge sums. It was a little trick her fellow students had mastered. She got off the bus slowly, as if she couldn't hold her body upright. She got to Café Danton more than fifteen minutes late and found Bruno sitting near a big glass window, across from another young man, who had his back turned to the entrance. That young man was Zeyad. She was a little hesitant walking over to the two of them. They stood up as she arrived, and Bruno introduced them. Then he stepped back from his chair, gesturing to Maya that she should sit in his place while saying, with a wide, ironic smile, "You must miss the war in Lebanon, I'm sure you'd like to hunt the people passing by on the other side of the window. Go on, take your weapon out of your purse and sit in my place. Just like it happens in Beirut. Just like a sniper on the roof of the Bourj al-Murr building."

His words irritated her and made her feel more stressed.

"I guess now you want to shoot a film about our war and you are thirsty to capture people's deaths and no longer interested in asking me about what I found in my research on Cairo. Isn't that so?" Maya answered with a sharpness Bruno wasn't used to and didn't understand. She wasn't expecting this kind of joking and she didn't want to react so harshly, but things had happened without her intending them to. Though she was convinced that Bruno hadn't meant to hurt her feelings, Maya felt that in this way he was equating her with the people who'd abducted Michel Seurat, whereas she saw them as a gang of murderers, nothing more. She felt even more stressed out because that Lebanese guy she'd just met started laughing aloud at Bruno's comment. Perhaps he hadn't heard her reaction. She expected such a conversation to annoy him, but it took her some time to discover that Zeyad rarely kept track of what was going on back in Lebanon, that he was distant from it all. He was trying to get French citizenship and settle in Paris. This, the first time they met, made little impression on her. From the comments Zeyad made during lunch, he seemed to her to be an unremarkable person.

5
BEIRUT, AUGUST 1994

She had to hurry; there wasn't even time to drink maté with her mother. Maya was astonished at how time passed so quickly in the morning. She ran from one place to another at home without finding her stuff: her shirt, lost in the closet, her black leather belt, left on the sofa yesterday had now disappeared ... the first draft of a chapter of her book about Asmahan; her diary; the notebook in which she'd written down part of a screenplay; the car keys; and that new invention, the mobile phone. Sometimes she felt she was searching in vain, that she'd never find her lost things. Shadi told her with painful innocence that her things must be angry with her because she didn't have time to play with them, that they'd gone out house hunting, looking for a new place to live. Maya knew that Shadi was using these words to describe himself; he wasn't referring to her things. Her friend Sarah was right when she told her that she couldn't carry on like this—Zeyad was dead, she had to accept his death and reestablish a peaceful life. Shadi needed her more than ever before, Sarah added. Since they'd returned to Beirut, Maya hadn't yet found even one full day to spend with Shadi or even a bit of time for them to play together. Without planning it beforehand, she'd entrusted him to her mother and his teacher at the daycare, as well as to Mala. Mala was a domestic worker who had come from Sri Lanka to Lebanon to earn a living for herself, her family, and her children, who missed her. After three years in Lebanon, she discovered that her husband had used the money she'd been sending to him in Sri Lanka to build a house and had married another woman, sending their children to live with her family. She decided to stay longer in Lebanon in order to recover this loss, then return to her children, who'd grown up in her absence and whose childhood she'd missed. Mala woke up early, drank tea, and waited for everyone else to wake up. This morning Maya felt a sudden pang of guilt when she saw Mala smiling, while carrying a tray with coffee for her and maté for Aida. When she finished, she started helping her search for her things, racing against time.

Maya dropped Shadi off at daycare, and then continued on her way to the Chase café in Achrafiyeh. She was meeting Danny to continue filming their documentary on the reconstruction of downtown Beirut. They were colleagues and they'd renewed their friendship since her return, after she'd had no news of him for the years she was living in Paris. Today he'd also have Ernest, his partner—in love and work— with him. They lived together in a flat in Sinn el-Fil. She parked the car in front of the post office and crossed the street to reach the café. She sat outside after ordering coffee and a croissant. It was a nice morning despite the August heat. She waited fifteen minutes, half an hour, but no one came. She took the phone out of her purse. She rang Danny.... No answer. *Perhaps he's still home,* she thought, but his home number wasn't stored in her phone. Maya took out her little book of addresses and phone numbers and found it. She rang him. It wasn't like him to be so late for a work appointment.

She dialed the number. Someone answered right away.

"Hello," she said.

"Hello," replied a man on the other end.

"Who's that? Is it Danny?" she asked.

"Who?" asked a puzzled voice.

"Could I speak to Danny or Ernest please?"

"Just a moment," he said hesitantly and gave the phone to someone else.

"Hello?" She heard another man's voice.

"Hello.... I would like to speak to Danny please. Or to Ernest if Danny's not there."

"Who are you looking for, Ma'am?"

"I'm looking for Danny."

"What number are you calling, Ma'am?"

"I'm calling 480-994.... Yes, that's it. What number are you?"

"We're in the suburbs, sister ... the southern suburbs.... All the numbers here start with 840, and there's no Ernest here and no Danny."

"Sorry.... So sorry to trouble you; I had the wrong number."

Maya put the mobile phone back into her purse, saying under her breath, "Damn you Danny and Ernest, and damn the damned telephone!" She took her papers back out to continue working. She decided to wait, since she couldn't really do anything else. She had to finish a short film on downtown Beirut for a company that would be doing reconstruction. From the beginning of her work on it, Maya found herself pursuing stories of people who were living in the capital, both downtown and in the surrounding neighborhoods. She followed their memories and their histories. Maya believed in the importance of doing interviews with them and including some of these in the film. She didn't understand why the company had asked her to document the memory of these places, without noticing that it was in fact completely erasing this memory. Maya didn't agree with Danny when he told her that it would be easy to use interviews as material serving the goal of the film. He added that making films is dangerous and clever work. Through the *montage*, he said, a director can assemble whatever he wants to say, and it's important not to waste time on long interviews with the residents there.

"That's right, it's a question of technique," Maya interrupted him. "But, it also goes beyond that, since it's impossible to separate the memory of a place from human memory. You know that listening to people and recording what they say is fundamental to my work."

Many minutes passed before she heard Danny's voice behind her, greeting her timidly but cheerfully. A stalled truck on the highway had caused a huge traffic jam. Ernest was standing near him silently, his hands in his shorts' pockets as if he were apologizing for a mistake, though it wasn't his fault. They looked like two boys late for school, fearing their punishment.

Maya looked at Danny with disapproval, and not without anger. "Our meeting was over an hour ago," she said in a firm but friendly way. She saw him smiling right at her, apologizing over and over again. Her anger subsided, and Danny and Ernest sat with her to drink coffee. She informed them about her conversation with the man in the southern suburbs. The tension dissipated and the three of them sank into laughter.

From the café they went to visit the apartment buildings near Riad El Solh Square going up toward Zuqaq al-Blat, then to the east toward Basta and the neighborhoods around Bechara El Khoury Street. The map they had with them seemed complete. The reconstruction sites had been set up and the bulldozers were working night and day, as were the preparations for the restoration projects. Martyrs' Square was full of merchants, other people, and the voices of children playing ball and shouting. One of the children answered Maya's question: "The bronze statue for the martyrs filled with bullet holes was for the martyrs of the Amal movement." Danny filmed the boy while he was speaking. They kept walking around downtown. There were areas along the streets there that they couldn't even go near because they hadn't been completely cleared of unexploded grenades and landmines, which militia fighters had put there to mark the borders between the warring groups. Personal belongings and ripped, broken furniture, which people had left behind when they fled, remained on the sidewalks, on mounds of dirt piled up here and there and in apartment buildings, most of which were occupied by fighters. Danny started filming, walking up the road that connected Riad El Solh Square with the surrounding neighborhoods. Devastated, deserted buildings were still standing, resisting their fall. The façade of an old, two-story building opposite them had fallen off a portion of the ground floor, blocking an apartment door, and the building roof was completely destroyed, fragile and naked, against the sky. The ground floor was otherwise intact.

The bulldozers started working that day around the building. After removing the rubble from in front of the entrance Maya was able to enter, and Danny filmed her and Ernest going inside. The camera was behind Maya, who was walking in front. She wasn't supposed to be in front of the camera, but Danny had a plan that took her by surprise—she would be in the frame during the filming. Part of the apartment door had blown off, and what remained was fixed with nails and held up by a large rock. Soil and sandbags and the rest of the household furnishings were scattered throughout the entryway, so Maya and the two men got inside with difficulty. The kitchen door at the end of the damp hallway was unscathed. A small stone staircase led upstairs from the kitchen. The kitchen had lost almost all of its contents: only a bit of its marble sink remained, hanging on the wall like a surreal painting. "It's so spacious, so large," Danny remarked. "Look at the ceiling—the colors of its paint and decorations have faded. My God, the ceiling needs a ladder with a hundred rungs to get up to it." Danny walked around a bit and then said that the place had been uninhabited for long time, so they should carry on filming in other places downtown. He turned to leave while Maya was busy discovering where the small stairs lead. "This is the attic!" she shouted in a loud voice that Danny, already back outside, couldn't hear. She was going up the edges of the stairs, dangling as though suspended in mid-air, the sound of her own heart beat resonating in her ears. Ernest walked behind her, leaving Danny to keep filming around the building and its entrance.

The attic floor was full of dust, dirt, decaying books, and old moldy newspapers. In the middle of the attic were the remnants of ashes, surrounded by human excrement and dead rats. A worn-out sneaker was upside-down in the corner, and the walls were covered with charcoal drawings with accompanying text in mostly black and red—among them, one of a naked woman with this written vertically between her thighs: "Death is here." Near this drawing were the words, "Abu Jamaajam lives on in us," and on the facing wall, "There is no god but God." Many words, religious and political slogans, names of militias—Maya tried in vain to read some of the faded letters. At the back of the attic was a long sofa with dirt and dust piled up on it. Next to it was a wrapped up, tattered blanket whose original color, which was difficult to discern, had transformed into dark brown. No doubt someone used to sleep here, Maya thought. Ernest approached and lifted the blanket, which become a worn out lump, and threw it onto the floor. Dust flew and both of them started coughing.

"Slow down!" Maya said, pinching her nose with two fingers. The sofa was the kind that had an empty wooden chest inside where you could store blankets and other things.

Maya indicated to Ernest that he should lift up the seat to see what was inside. Immediately a rotten odor filled the air. Dirt, junk, and little, desiccated, dead animals filled the sofa's belly. In one of the corners was a small, faded, brown leather suitcase—the kind you might carry on board an airplane—covered in dirt and ripped open on one side. Fabrics wrapped up in a little ball were hanging out from under it. Yellowed papers were scattered around it. Maya tried to dislodge it and lift it up, wondering what was inside. Danny now started calling up to them from in front of the building, urging them to come out. Ernest stood looking at Maya, who was completely taken by what she had found; he was hesitating between the two of them. Should he stay with her or go back to Danny? He left Maya at Danny's insistence, and started slowly descending the staircase, shouting again and again that he was coming. Meanwhile Maya had gotten the little suitcase out and put it on the ground. It was difficult to open, since its metal locks on both sides had rusted, so it was hard even to move them at all. But after a struggle, she managed to open the suitcase to find rolls of stuck-together paper, large pieces of which had been consumed by humidity. Reading them would require more than just daylight, which barely reached the attic's tiny, dirt-covered window. This was a moment of fear, as much as of excitement and the discovery of the unknown. "I won't leave it here," Maya said to herself. "No! Maybe this is what I've been searching for. Maybe I'll find stories of people who have passed on, and this the only trace or evidence of their lives. Who knows, maybe this suitcase has been waiting for years for me to come and bring what's in it out into the light of day."

Despite the faint light, Maya could see, among the papers, envelopes containing letters and photos whose color had been affected by humidity that made them stick together in a single pile. She could barely make out the things at the bottom of the suitcase. A semidisintegrated cotton t-shirt, small pieces of fabric that seemed like children's clothes, a key ring, newspapers clippings, small notebooks whose covers had lost their original colors. She put everything back into the suitcase, locked it again, brushed the dust off of it, and carried it down the stone staircase leading to the spacious kitchen. Walking down the stairs, she was like an apparition falling from the sky, her face and hair a bank of thick clouds, a dull, mud color covering her clothes.

It was almost three in the afternoon and they hadn't had lunch yet. Ernest and Danny walked toward Bechara El Khoury Street, where there was a simple little falafel place. Maya didn't want to go with them, fearing she would be late picking up Shadi from daycare. Carrying the suitcase, she walked to her car, which was parked quite far from where they were. She took the street going up the hill, in the middle of the mounds of dirt and gravel that covered the roads, so she could get to the main road. She was excited at the thought of the booty she'd found and wanted to hurry home to start reading. While hurrying to her car, Maya called Sarah and reported the most salient among the contents of the suitcase: a treasure-trove of damp papers and faded ink, darkened photos and newspaper clippings, all of it gathering dust and dirt. She put the suitcase in the trunk, sat down, and started the car. She had to get to the school as quickly as possible; it was three-thirty and Shadi would be waiting for her. But how would she get there in the middle of this daily Beirut torture they call "traffic"?

Maya opened all the windows to let out the heat trapped inside the car. It was August, and Beirut was getting unbearable. She thought about her clothes, almost all of which were dirty, and remembered that there was no electricity just now to run the washing machine. No, the power came on only late at night, when she was already sleeping, and what electricity that reached their apartment from the generator wouldn't be enough for the washer. She thought about the stuff in their house in France, things she would have liked to have with her—antique books she'd collected while living there, some of which she had restored parts of, and the newspaper articles and books she had gathered about the life and death of Asmahan. Maya thought about moving all of it to Beirut and the huge expense, which she couldn't afford. She had to get herself together to enroll Shadi in school, to rent a little place for the two of them, and to ... the list was long and unending. Right now she was living with her mother in the family house until she found a solution. But did she have to think about all this, she wondered, now at this very moment, in this unbearable traffic?

Shadi sat in the backseat. He told her that today he drew a picture of the sky and the sun that the teacher hung up on the wall, and that she stamped his hand with a gold star. He held his hand out proudly to show his mother the star. She looked at his hand quickly, made some happy sounding noises, and then turned back around, avoiding the cars accelerating to pass her on both sides. *In Beirut, driving is not an art but sheer madness,* she said to herself.

Maya parked the car in a space not too far from the house. She could almost taste the smell of fried falafel wafting out from a small restaurant. "Shouldn't I stay in Beirut just for this smell?" she asked herself and smiled. The man sitting behind the cash register exchanged smiles with her, repeating her order aloud, "Two sandwiches with a lot of vegetables and sauce for Madame...."

In the evening, she left Shadi on the floor of his room playing with colored LEGOs, building a big house, and telling his grandma, Aida, "This is our house in Paris." Maya reflected that Shadi would have childhood memories of another place, a place that held no memories of her childhood. His home was there and not here. She sat on the balcony off the kitchen and opened the suitcase she'd found in the ruined apartment. She began by taking everything out of it. She put the papers that were in good condition in a cardboard box. From time to time, she wiped the dust off with a small towel and read every page whose words were still clear enough. There were many names of anonymous people; personal letters, most of which were in English; pictures; and a notepad with Noura Abu Sawwan's name on it; an address book; a thick diary; keys on a rusted metal keychain; an identity card; an expired travel document; articles from Arabic and non-Arabic journals and newspapers about the Russian pioneer astronaut Yuri Gagarin; as well as other things.

Maya had to prepare a plan for the next day's filming, and yet she had forgotten the film, her work, and the whole project. This suitcase and its contents preoccupied her, as though the goal of everything she had ever done was to find this suitcase and now she had finally found it. She was completely immersed in reading what was inside; the many names on the back of the photos occupied her thoughts, as did those which appeared in the letters and diaries: Noura Abu Sawwan, Henaa Abu Sawwan, Huda, Shawqi, Shahani, Kemal Firat, Sabah Karabouz, Fawziya Karabouz, Ahmad Karabouz, Atta, Taymour, Suhayl, and the rest of them. It was as if Maya were waiting to take these names out of darkness and silence. The story had found someone to tell it. But who was this Sabah? Who was Kemal? Noura? Taymour? Who was this Ahmad, whose name occurred less often than the others? She put the letters aside to look at the many photos, most of them black and white; a few, color. Names were written on the back of the photos in what seemed to be a child's handwriting. Then she turned to the letters in a big envelope, which bore three handwritten words: "Letters from Istanbul." From there she went back to flipping through Noura Abu Sawwan's diary, which filled two notebooks, both of which were covered in construction paper. These diaries reflected the full life of their author. She went back to the letters again, love letters Kemal Firat had written to Noura Abu Sawwan in English, with some sentences in Arabic and Turkish, most of them sent from Istanbul.

Each of the letters was dated, unlike the diaries, few of which had a specific day or month written on their pages. Most of what Maya found had been written in the middle of the 1970s. The name of the letters' author was repeated more than once in the woman's diary. "But who is this woman?" Maya wondered again. The woman wrote about her adolescence, and then about coming to Lebanon. She wrote about meeting Kemal and about her rich and confused life in Damascus and Beirut before they met. Then there was her documentation of the life of Yuri Gagarin, the Russian pioneer astronaut who was killed in mysterious circumstances, so that she could write a book about him. "No doubt she was some kind of writer," Maya reflected. But she'd never heard of her before, nor had she read any books about Gagarin that had her name on them. And why had she chosen Gagarin? Maya wondered. It was funny that Maya in particular would think this since she herself had devoted so much time in Paris to searching for old, out-of-print books and to collecting articles about the life of Asmahan, who had died in similarly mysterious circumstances to Gagarin.

Maya found the name Sabah Karabouz on one of the old yellow envelopes, as well as an address in Beirut: The Kh ... y ... building, Khandaq al-Ghamiq. The name of the building was not completely clear. It started with the letter "kh," with a dot above it, an "h" with no dot, or perhaps it was a "j" with the dot below.... The wear of years had eaten away at the letters in the middle. To figure out the name of the unknown building, Maya added one letter of the alphabet at a time to the "kh." In most of her attempts the word sounded odd, as if taken from an Agatha Christie novel.

It was a long night; Maya didn't remember the number of times she moved back and forth between the kitchen balcony and the living room sofa. Nor did she remember what time after dawn she moved to her bedroom, swaying while walking as if intoxicated. She only remembered that she sat in bed and kept reading Kemal's letters to Noura.

A large picture of Asmahan was still hanging on the wall opposite her bed, in the same place it had been since her university days. Maya's childhood friend Sarah had given it to her on her eighteenth birthday. Sarah knew how much Asmahan meant to her friend and that she always listened to her songs. At the beginning of the war in Lebanon, before Maya left for France, this picture of Asmahan was one of the few things that could still dispel her feelings of loneliness.

She didn't sleep for practically the entire night—not only because of Beirut's summer heat and humidity with no electricity, but also because of the letters and diary she'd found in the suitcase and that she'd kept reading by candlelight after the generator stopped working at midnight. Maya kept moving from one page to the next, reading then stopping and getting up from her chair to walk to the edge of the balcony and feel a bit of the gentle breeze. What annoyed her most was when she couldn't read a whole letter because humidity had faded its ink and eaten away at the paper. She could restore parts of some letters, but others were completely ruined.

Maya kept reading all night. She had to move repeatedly from Kemal Firat's letters to Noura Abu Sawwan's diary to connect the dates and events in order for the story to unfold. With the early morning light, she made a pot of coffee, her body feeling like a machine as it moved between the balcony and the kitchen.

While lighting her morning cigarette, Maya resolved

to herself that this very week she would begin to search for that incomplete address in Khandaq al-Ghamiq and for the woman named Sabah. Perhaps she would first phone Danny to postpone their filming to another day.

Then she went back to read more of the Letters from Istanbul....

6
LETTERS FROM ISTANBUL

Istanbul
7 December 1975

Dear Noura,

During your visit to Istanbul and our first meeting, you asked me to write you part of my life story. I promised you that I would write though I didn't know (and I still don't know now) why I accepted and promised you this: I would have preferred to continue our conversation face to face. But I trust that what you are doing will support us here in Turkey and what we tell you will reach many readers here and throughout the world. Therefore, I am now going to do what I promised you. Forgive me if my first letter to you isn't in chronological order. I will write down what my memory can help me with, and forgive me if the stories and events I mention here weave through the corridors of time with childish petulance.

One afternoon when I had not yet turned eight, my father was getting his haircut at the neighborhood barber's in Izmir when a military jeep arrived. Two soldiers got out, went into the barbershop, and arrested him. We didn't know where they had taken him until four days later. He was put in solitary confinement because he belonged to the outlawed communist party. The situation in military Turkey boiled over when Prime Minister Adnan Menderes abolished laws relating to language and the azaan that had been implemented by the Ataturk regime. My father and many others were victims of the political conflicts in the Turkey of the fifties. My father was in prison for ten years when I was growing up, and I went abroad to France during this time to study with a government grant I was awarded by the Lycée Français. His imprisonment shaped my entire life. At the time it happened I couldn't have known that one day my political affiliations would be similar to my father's. When I finished my studies in Paris, I returned to Turkey to become the editor responsible for the political division of Agence France Presse (AFP). As for my father, he left prison half-broken, ill, and an alcoholic.

In the early years of my adolescence, I dreamed a lot. I dreamed of one day returning to my grandfather's house in Antakia. Oh, have you seen how I jump from one time period to another? My family came from Antakia, meaning my grandfather's family's house was there. After the First World War, we became Turks overnight. There was no place to go. My grandfather thought of moving to Syria but the family decided to stay just like everyone else. My grandfather insisted on teaching my father and his brother Arabic. So did my grandmother, who spoke Kurdish as well as Arabic. My father was Turkish, but his mother was of Syrian Kurdish origin. I grew up between three languages, all of which I spoke, though the schools forbade any language other than Turkish. My family moved around between the different regions of Turkey because of my father's employment, or, better put, his unemployment. I was born in Izmir, lived my childhood years and adolescence near the sea, and we changed houses a lot in Izmir. After my father's imprisonment, we moved to Istanbul, where my mother's brother lived.

My father always dreamed of one homeland for all of us, a homeland that would be for all Turks, Kurds, and Armenians, whatever nation or country they came from. A place distinguished by cultural riches would make our lives more humane. Turkey has a lot of ethnicities and a long history of bloody struggles as well. It is enough to tell my family's stories from both my mother and father's sides to demonstrate how difficult it is to meld all the people here together under one common umbrella of a unified cultural identity. I believe that what I am writing to you about Turkey applies in some ways to the other countries in the region, too. Ataturk wanted to build a nation but it was done at the expense of people's freedoms and the expense of many ethnic and minority groups whose identities and destinies were changed by force and violence that took many different shapes. Do you believe that the massacres suffered by the Armenians at the beginning of the century were the end of the crimes of our modern history? Not at all. When a regime starts to make such bloody choices, stopping is difficult—indeed impossible.

It grows accustomed to violence and finds it an easy solution. History tells us this, even when this violence is committed on a smaller scale backstage. Do you know what it means to forbid a person to speak a language they know, when they haven't yet reached the age of ten? This is what happened to my father. A law was issued in the year 1934 that forced people to speak Turkish, to change their family names to fit into Ataturk's new nationalism. My grandfather was not allowed to speak Kurdish, which his mother had taught him at home. The same was true for Arabic, which his grandmother had taught him. It's as if homelands can only be built at the expense of ordinary people. This fact isn't written down in history books! Our generation was raised on songs about the glorification of the homeland, the homeland that killed us in its name, and was built on victory with no place in it for the vanquished. I discovered that this "homeland," my dear Noura, extends its life through power and denial of the other, so I hated it.

It would seem that I have become like my father, despite my hatred for him as well. I dream of a homeland where I can raise my children, plant trees, go fishing, and befriend my neighbor, who doesn't look like me or speak my language, my neighbor from whom I can learn about a different culture. I dream of a place with no wars or weapons. But I know that my dream is impossible and that if I become a father, I will be forced one day to teach my son to carry weapons to defend himself and his difference, because he won't feel he belongs either to the military or to those who dream about reclaiming the glory of the wretched Ottoman Empire by transforming

Turkey into a religious project. But I don't want this to be my son's destiny. I don't want him to have to resort to violence in order to survive. Despite this, I will tell him my grandfather's story and his grandfather's story and the stories of those peaceful, brave people they mistreated, uprooted, and put in prison.

My grandfather spoke many languages and called all of them his "mother" tongue. He spoke Arabic fluently. I still remember the song he sang to us as children when he lived in our house for a while: "Brr brr, it's cold…. I don't have any kindling for firewood, but I have a little girl, she's playing the drums." I also listened to my mother singing—sometimes in Kurdish and sometimes in Turkish—to my sister, who was born three years after me.

The male infants my mother gave birth to all died just weeks after they were born. They said my father's family was responsible—that the Antankia curse had followed them. This was a family curse from a young man my father's uncle had killed for no reason. He had been forced to flee before the two families might have come to an agreement such as a payment of blood money. When I was born, my mother lied, telling everyone she'd had a girl until I reached the age of four. She addressed me as a girl, dressed me in skirts, grew my hair long, and put earrings on me. She felt compelled to do this because she believed what an old Roma woman had told her, that my mother wouldn't have male children because they would all die shortly after birth.

Maybe both because of this and also the absence of my father, I sometimes say that the feeling of masculinity—that cocky young man's feeling about himself, the feeling that he owns a woman—didn't develop in me. Indeed, I really used to want to be a woman, despite my strong feelings of sexual desire for women. Perhaps this isn't what you wanted to know about me, at least not at the moment!

In Izmir, when I was four years old, we moved from my grandfather's house to a house only for us. I was wearing a girl's dress, my father was carrying a big, colorful suitcase, and my mother was carrying my little sister. After we moved there, my mother changed my clothes, dressing me normally, in clothes like those the other little boys in the neighborhood wore: traditional sirwal trousers and a loose shirt. We lived in a working-class area inhabited by Turks who had emigrated there from the countryside, most of them peasants from remote areas—both Turks and Kurds—and some people from Syria. Our house was composed of two adjoining rooms; we used to eat and sit in the room that we slept in. The other room was for my father's entertaining at night. I liked our house, because as soon as I went out onto the road I would quickly reach my uncle's house right on the seafront. I used to leave my little rowboat there, the one my father had bought me just after my seventh birthday. I would go out fishing with my uncle in that boat. I loved the sea and I loved Izmir. In our new house, my mother started working as a playground monitor at the Lycée Français Saint Joseph, where I also studied. Every day she'd then come home, cook, and clean.

The year ended and my father's comrades gathered in our house: pandemonium, thick smoke, and booze. My father drank raki until he got so drunk that he slurred his words. But this didn't stop him from making fun of my mother in front of his friends whenever she brought them something she'd cooked for them.

I covered my head with my duvet in bed so the noise wouldn't reach me and I wouldn't hear what he was saying. I felt my mother's hand on my head, and she kissed me, saying, "Don't let happiness escape you." I covered my eyes, dreamed of a new year, and said that happiness was hiding at the end of the year that would end in a few hours; I thought that this time I had to search hard for happiness and not let it escape me. I became a happiness hunter, though I could never catch it. My mother taught me to read and write before I went to school, even to write my name in more than one language. She had been my father's communist party comrade. After marriage, though, she turned into a wife and mother.

My uncle was a better man than my father; he used to visit us all the time, camera in hand. All the photos I have of myself as a child were taken by my uncle. He liked to photograph my mother, saying she had a face the camera liked. My uncle surely had deep, warm feelings for my mother, and sometimes visited her to photograph her even when my father wasn't there. My mother never liked her photos. I think she didn't like them because in most of them we surrounded her, my sister and me next to my father. For a long time my mother hated those of her pictures that included my father and us. There is something sad in her eyes, in those pictures, that is still part of me to this day. Continual unease shadowed her face as if she existed in two states of being at the same time: One was that of a woman who dreams of having something that is hers alone and needs only the wings to fly. The other is that of a submissive woman with an unchanging fate. She didn't want to hang any photos of her with the family on the wall or put them on the table at home. I remember what she said once when she looked at one of them: "Even in pictures I have to suffer him being there." She was referring to my father.

My father increased his party activism after my mother found work with a decent income. The first job he did was to distribute party leaflets in the street, until the Turkish army arrested him for it, as I mentioned at the beginning of this letter. When the soldiers came to arrest him I had just come home from school. They didn't find him, though, so they went inside and turned everything upside down: the beds, cupboards, bookshelves with my schoolbooks and my father's political books. They ripped up all the books and asked my mother where the weapons were hidden. "Weapons?" my mother asked angrily. "With everything that you are doing to us, who would dare to keep weapons in his house?"

They shot and killed my dog Baroud, who had started barking when he saw them enter the house with their weapons and heavy boots. One of them aimed his gun at him and it took only one bullet to kill him. Baroud tipped over onto the ground as his barks turned into a whimper.

Writing is difficult. It isn't nothing; it doesn't just come from nowhere! Pain is present even in just remembering. What is my state of being when this pain is transforming into words and images right before me? I can't ignore my trauma. It is here, I feel it every single moment; I've started to believe that forgetfulness is mercy.

After the soldiers stopped, went out, and left my mother hitting her head with her hands, she tried to save what she could of our damaged furniture. Fear had gotten my sister's tongue and she hid in her bed crying.... When I reached my hand out to touch the head of my dog Baroud, dying in front of the door, it made me feel an overwhelming desire to scream, but I didn't. I couldn't cry.

At the beach, they destroyed my little boat, smashing it into small pieces scattered on the sand. They didn't leave anything unbroken; this was the region's military. I'm sure you know what I'm talking about—you come from a country where a family seized power and now governs through repression and mukhabarat.

I grew up that day and was no longer a boy. I grew up in one fell swoop. Anger made me a man who wanted to settle accounts and take revenge ... a man who experienced humiliation, shame, and helplessness, when faced with a brute force that knew no compassion or justice. That anger took away the Kemal I was.

I admit that the one thing that made me feel less sad that day is that they had put my father in prison, that he wouldn't be coming home that evening. My mother, my little sister, and I would maybe be able to have more peace and quiet at home. My communist father attended meetings and discussions, gave speeches, and demanded both women's rights and improvements in the conditions of workers and the poorer classes. But when he came home, he swore and demanded he be treated like a king, not only by my mother but also by his children. This contradiction scared me and made me feel unsafe. In fact, my father used to be scared of my mother, as she was taller than him and physically stronger, too. He swore at her in a low voice so the guests wouldn't hear, then wink at me as if he wanted me to conspire with him against her. He was a coward but very intelligent. It was the same intelligence that characterizes a wounded fox: he knew how to take revenge on her through various means, usually in social situations so she would be forced to stay silent in order to avoid endless gossip among the neighbors and in the area. I didn't love my father but perhaps now I should be more compassionate when I write about him. Despite all this, he never lost himself—he didn't betray his comrades or become a spy for the Turkish security apparatus after he got out of jail. I didn't want to become a communist like my father. Maybe this was because of my belief that all communists were like that—outside the house they played at being militants, discussing and debating, and inside it they returned to their true nature, filled with bad temper and the desire to control. But life propels us to places we never expected it would and destinies we haven't planned for. When I turn to the past, I think the person I am now has definitively parted ways with the child I was then. The warmth I felt deep inside me while waiting for the New Year was merely a dream; it ended without me knowing it.

I'll stop there.

Faithfully yours,

Kemal Firat

**

Istanbul
18 February 1976

My dear Noura,

Perhaps you were wondering about the reason for my delay in writing you a second letter, despite your short reply that I got through the press agency (AFP). I was waiting for Taymour's trip to Beirut so I could send a letter with him; surely you remember him. Perhaps I didn't tell you when you met him in Istanbul that he is my colleague in the agency and a friend I trust and rely on for many things. You will surely meet him more than once.

Happy about the news of your upcoming visit to Istanbul during the spring holiday. The weather here will have improved and it will be a good opportunity to meet again. As to your question, unfortunately you won't find any of my articles for AFP translated into English, and of course you won't find them in Arabic either. We live in neighboring countries and neither can read the other's language. It's only the mukhabarat in each country that can, but so they can spy—not to improve our neighborly relations. But at least I can follow what you do on your BBC radio programs that are sometimes translated into English. I ask you to keep my name, as well as that of my comrades in the Turkish resistance, anonymous on your program. This is a sensitive issue and you know the implications here, with the increase in measures taken against the opposition every day, especially after the 1971 military coup, during and after which many comrades in factories and universities were imprisoned. I sometimes feel that we fell right into a trap with three sharp teeth: the authorities in Moscow, the American-backed military, and the terrifying rise of religion. In the end, I see these three forces as similar in keeping Turkey in the grip of oppression and the silencing of freedom of expression. Turkish history is changing, so is the history of the region; I see enormous avalanches coming. We have to find our voice, distinct from those deadly traps, though we know the risks we are facing on all sides and the cost of what lies ahead.

What's coming to us over the wires where I work about what's happening in Lebanon is not reassuring. I don't feel good about it. Take care of yourself and please let Taymour know the date and time of your upcoming trip to Istanbul. I am eager to welcome you.

A kiss atop your head for now, as I await our meeting,

Kemal

Istanbul
20 April 1976

Noura,

The two weeks we spent together in Istanbul changed my life. Is this what happiness is? Is this love? I've never experienced it before, though I am more than thirty years old. It's as if I have spent all that time waiting for you, you who are timeless. [...]

When you left, I found myself alone. The feelings that filled me were like the first day I went to school: feelings of abandonment and loneliness, which I had to face up to. Remembering all of these things in my life now after you left has let me see how much your short visit here connected me to you. [...]

When we meet next time, I will tell you about my dreams, even the craziest ones that could become real if you agree. I'm waiting for you all the time faithfully and patiently.

Let me kiss you on both your eyes

**

Istanbul
2 May 1976

Noura,
[...]

I believe in you and the journey of your soul. There are sailors who travel, leaving the port of their return behind them. They travel in the archipelagoes of their dreams. They are like us, my love. I think of you and love you always. The telephone now only means hearing your voice, nothing else. Reading your words is a balsam for the pain engendered by separation.

I'm scribbling these few words to you as Taymour waits for me. I'm writing you with the shawl you left here on the bed the day you traveled back to Beirut wrapped around my neck. I rub it against my face, I inhale your scent deeply, and I know how much I love you.

[…]

Kemal

**

Istanbul
2 May 1976

Noura,

[…]

And so I'm waiting for next week, and I can no longer stand the wait. I haven't put down my ticket for days. I am dreaming of us being together. I have so much to tell you about in Beirut.

[…]

Istanbul
14 June 1976

Noura,

[…]

… Your body embraces me with light, the light of your glowing skin, a blue halo surrounding us and our bed. Isn't this the "fourth impossible" they talk about in Arabic legends: to find each other, despite our geographical and social distance, with you in one country and me in another? This is love—I have been waiting for you for hundreds of years. I am waiting for you, you who are as timeless as the oceans.

This is the meaning of happiness. This is what so many of us can't express very well, until it has become the past. But I see it in the present and in the future.

You told me, my love, that you don't have a description of happiness. But I know when it is love. Love is always linked to doubt, fear, and uncertainty, but when you are propelled toward someone else without anyone forcing you to be, then it is happiness. It is a desire to be there, in that state of love. To be with the one you love.

It is that desire to be where we are, to be where we are powerfully, the desire to be together, here in this very moment, present.

Coming back to the words of Maulana Jalal al-din al Rumi that I whispered to you in Beirut:

"This is how I would die into the love I have for you: as pieces of cloud dissolve in the sunlight."

[…]

I am waiting for you in Istanbul.

Istanbul
25 July 1976

My love,

Your absence is painful. I told myself this morning that this house, whose threshold no woman but you has crossed, needs

you here. Every room in it contains your fingerprints; its air carries your scent. I console myself by saying that your absence from it now is not emptiness. This absence is present, but less burdensome: the shirt you left hanging in the cupboard with my clothes, your photo next to my bed—the one I took of you standing in front of our old house in Istanbul. I wanted to photograph you there so that you could enter right into the heart of not merely my present and future but also my past.
[…]

I'm going to sleep now; I'll search for your eyes and find them in my dreams.

My heart is overwhelmed by your presence,

Kemal

**

Istanbul
8 September 1976

[…]
I hear the news from Lebanon and wonder if the Syrian regime took a decision to swallow up Lebanon's remaining autonomy, with the blessing of the Arabs and perhaps the rest of world too. I expect dark days ahead.…
[…] I'm afraid for you and want us to be together.

I am leaving for Izmir now. Whenever I want to be by myself I leave Istanbul for Izmir. It's where I was born. I need to see the sea. You will tell me, "Istanbul has the sea, too." But

it's only the sea in Izmir that brings me back to myself, to connecting with the depths of my soul. We will surely go there
together, my love. I *lived* the sea, I feel that I am from the
sea; it's the doorway to my passion for life. I'm sending you a
picture. This is the beach near our house; the sea is a picture
of life. It always rules over everything and wins. When I feel
lost I return there, where the sea takes me back to what it
taught me over and over again. In life, as in the sea, I only
have to know how to steer a ship. I have to respect the wind
and not trust a stupid god or cruel, false prophet. Rather, I
have to search for authentic human nature, equal parts spirit
and matter. I'm writing all this thinking of us together. Do
you think of me, too? This ancient equation is the compass of
love—the desires of two people, coming together. Then, with
this equation in mind, we can understand how to navigate
difficult seas. We'll learn how to steer the ship well, through
winds and storms, and sometimes in their absence....

I will try to call you today, as usual. How I love the words
"as usual"! I want my life with you to be like this—as usual,
every day.

[...]

I kiss your two eyes and your lips,

Yours,

Kemal

Istanbul
13 November 1976

Noura,
[...]
On our last day, when I saw you turning over to get out of bed, I desired you at that moment once again. A painful desire. Looking at your naked body ignited in me a mixture of lust and melancholy—and a tingling deep inside me—as if by turning around in this way your two bare feet were stomping on my heart, walking all over my body. I felt like you were leaving me somehow.

I didn't want you to return to Beirut this time. I really wanted you to stay here longer. Meeting, separation, and meeting again makes me feel out of control. I want to always remain encircled by your scent. It still fills the house so you are here in some way.

Kissing your ten scrumptious toes,
[...]

Istanbul
5 December 1976

Noura ...

It is midnight here ... and you are there. I didn't get my fill from our call. I am giving you the pleasure of the world now. Accept it only with love and kindness. I feel your generosity here, despite your absence. I in turn will accept your love at the very same moment. It is love that transforms us into gods.

[…]

Istanbul
2 April 1977

My love,
[…]
… and in Cairo I went to Khan al-Khalili. I saw a perfume maker there selling perfumes in cheerfully colorful, delicate glass bottles that were arranged on the shelves with striking beauty.

I smelled a perfume in one of those little bottles, one reflecting rainbow colors. I pointed to it, indicating I wanted it. Suddenly I heard the perfume maker asking me, in English, with a charming Egyptian accent, "How much you want, sir, Is fifty grams of paradise enough?"

"Fifty grams of paradise!" I repeated, laughing with joy at his question. "Fifty grams of paradise!"

He said grams and not milliliters…. What does it matter, I told myself. It's enough that he offered me paradise, and what he offered me, my love, was a lot … a lot. Only one drop of our paradise together is enough for me.

[…]

Istanbul
12 September 1977
[...]
I have crossed the border between Turkey and Syria, as well as Turkey and Iraq, many times.... It's strange how the borders vary between a rugged, mountainous geography on the one side and an expansive desert on the other. I crossed the desert once and the silence was like no other. You told me once, my love, that through the silence I could hear the voice of your desire. Your desire rings out inside of you when you miss me and want me. I remember when you told me this. I felt that it truly was the voice of desire. This voice brings me closer to God. Actually, it's God's voice.

Istanbul
24 October 1977
[...]
I'm lost since my return from Beirut. My days only count when we've been together. I ask myself why, up until now, haven't you left Beirut and come to live here. Will you continue on like this?

I recall now what you said about each one of us having our own black hole.

Since we met, my darling, my black hole has become a colorful garden....
[...]

Istanbul
23 November 1977

My love,

We have so much to talk about when we meet: you moving from Beirut and your work here in Istanbul. Remember what we discussed on the telephone yesterday. We have to choose either the destination or the speed. We can't have both together. Don't worry about the difference in language here, my love, we've already overcome this since meeting. We're part of the same region. The military, mukhabarat mentality is the same—the same oppression, the same despotism—even if it happens in a different language. We have our own language, determined not by place but by our love.
[…]
    Death is creeping toward the Middle East. Violence is spreading. But we will be together.
    I am awaiting your arrival impatiently.
[…]

Istanbul
1 March 1978

Love slows down time. Either it makes us not feel time passing … or time is what makes us no longer able to feel love.
    I read your letter many times. Yes, my darling, the war is endless and it's not stopping; optimism is bravery that many

people around us lack. As you wrote in your story about your sister Henaa: hope needs brave people.

I won't pressure you further, even though I want you to leave Beirut today, not tomorrow. But you should only leave of your own volition, with less a sense of loss and deprivation.
[…]

Istanbul
15 March 1978

My love,
[…]
… I am following what is happening in South Lebanon. Until now no news has reached us of any attempts by the Syrian army to respond to Israel's Operation Litani, even though the Syrian army is occupying Lebanese territory! I wonder what they're doing there, then! Your office manager told me what you think about all this. But I now agree with him that your going to the South is mad.

I'm worried about you. Don't put yourself and the baby inside you in danger. You two are my life.
[…]

Istanbul
[no date]

… I know that my letter will perhaps never arrive, but I'm

writing you nonetheless, even though your phone line in Beirut is cut off, the airport is closed, and going to you is impossible. I am writing to you. Even though all the roads are blocked, my love, I will imagine us together—the rain that I hear now, we are hearing together, we're listening to it in our bed. I will imagine you smiling when you read the words "our bed," and you telling me that it "hasn't become our bed yet, it is still your bed and your bed alone." But, my darling, I don't have anything that's not for you, everything I have is yours. When I look for furniture for the house here in Istanbul, I think that it is ours, both of ours.

I kiss every little part of your body. Kiss our baby for me, our love that is growing inside you.

[…]

Istanbul
5 May 1978
[…]
… I started to write about the tenth anniversary of May 1968…. It's as if it were yesterday. But I stopped. I was studying in Paris at the time and preparing to return to Istanbul. We didn't know then that the movement we believed in— that would change the world—would be choked off after such a short period of time. How much has the situation changed since then? Nothing remains of that anniversary, except 69…!
[…]

Istanbul

15 June 1978

[…]

The last time we made love, who would have thought that you were pregnant?

Now you are far away, my love, but despite this we are together. This is the first time you've said you're convinced of the idea of leaving Beirut. I've been waiting for you to say those words. We will meet soon.

I promise you.

[…]

Istanbul

10 July 1978

Some comrades were jailed at dawn this morning. It's getting stressful here, my love. I'm almost afraid to walk to the Agency (AFP). They are following us. I wanted to cultivate hope here in Istanbul, but I am forced to leave the city tomorrow or the next day for Izmir, and such circumstances make it impossible to return. As we agreed on the phone in our last conversation, you have to leave Lebanon, but I no longer feel safe here. We will find another place, outside Turkey. If he is able to travel this week, Taymour will update you on everything. At the first opportunity, I'll try to slip across to Beirut from Izmir to see you, so that we can organize our exit together. I'll try to prepare the papers at the French embassy here. I expect you to tell me that you are going to feel alienated if we travel to a third country you have never been to, but the feeling of alienation in our own countries is more humiliating than it is in any other place. [...]

I'll let my head rest in the place nearest to what's living inside you, and I'll feel your hands in my hair, my face stuck to your warmer, wetter places. I need you.

[...]

7

KHANDAQ AL-GHAMIQ, AUGUST 1994

"I can't sleep.... What was the point of that visit?"

Sabah was talking to herself, tossing and turning in bed on the ground floor of the building in Khandaq al-Ghamiq. She meant Maya's visit to her the previous afternoon. It wasn't the heat that woke her up this time, but anxiety throbbing inside her and hurting her head. Numbers flashed before her closed eyes, as if she were still asleep and having a disturbing nightmare. Sounds, events, and words of Noura's that Sabah believed she'd forgotten were repeating and ringing in her head. Men in camouflage gear passed in front of her, stopped near her bed, and then left. Military boots, putrid odors, and hidden screaming. She hung her feet off the bed while searching for her medicine among the little cardboard boxes strewn across the small table. She found the Xanax on the floor near the head of the bed; she took a pill, swallowing it without water. This eased her headache a little and also calmed her anxiety. Sabah believed that this headache had pursued her since menopause began to set in.

"Every time I see the doctor, he tells me I have depression. What is this never-ending illness?" she said that morning, standing and looking at things scattered all around her bed. Stuff everywhere. Piles of clothes, plastic bags full of things that she believed she might need someday, but that had been thrown here for years. A chair that needed repairing, a broken mirror, picture frames she had found one day by the side of the road, a folded curtain torn down the middle, little plastic boxes, empty flowerpots, a broken telephone; and a pile of newspapers and magazines, some of which had in them a faded, black-and-white picture of a man. On the wall near her bed, Sabah had hung a picture of her disappeared husband, and she'd stuck plastic carnations around its frame.

She always thought that she should tidy up her house and organize the stuff she no longer needed, but whenever she'd be about to start cleaning, her back pain would recur and all she'd do in the end was sit and wait. She waited for whichever one would return first—Ahmad her husband or Ahmad her old boyfriend—and thought about the blood bond between herself and Ahmad her boyfriend, about the vow that they would stay together for a lifetime. She asked, "What happened to him?" As if love's days were numbered. They'd finish, going bad as quickly as the fruit of a mulberry tree. Meows came from the garden of her ground-floor apartment, the cat's claws scratching the kitchen door. This was her only visitor. Sabah, half-naked because of the summer heat, wrapped her large, summer abaya around her body, gathered her dyed-blonde hair up in a clip, and moved swaying from the cramped bedroom to the little living room. Then she forgot what she'd wanted to do there. She turned around and went into the kitchen, muttering unintelligible words to express some kind of discomfort. She stood in the narrow corridor staring for a while at the big black-and-white poster on the wall. It was a picture of the pioneering Russian cosmonaut Yuri Gagarin. Its edges had yellowed and part of it was ripped. She stared into Gagarin's face as he was smiling through the window of his ship. Then she went in the kitchen. She opened the wooden door onto the little garden where she found the cat, which had lived there for years and still had no name, looking at her. Every day, Sabah expected the cat to leave and never return. Like both her boyfriend Ahmad and her husband Ahmad. Like everyone she had ever loved in her life—Noura and her child, Kemal and Taymour, Khawaja Ibrahim, and her last remaining girlfriend, Mariam. Mariam was the last one to go, and Sabah had continued to visit her throughout her illness; she gave her money to buy food. Mariam could no longer walk well. When Sabah visited her, she could do nothing but lie in bed, a transistor radio on a low table beside her. Mariam sold practically all the furniture in her house, piece by piece. Only one painting that she used to have remained. Then she had nothing at all. Sabah went over the names of everyone she had lost by death or travel abroad. An invisible thread separated death and travel, which made her not good at remembering the reason each person was gone.

All of these people had left, and Sabah didn't want to get attached to this cat that was meowing in her garden or to give her a name. Just so the cat too could leave before Sabah even picked her up and stroked her soft fur, before

85

Sabah kissed her and loved her. Sabah wouldn't let her come in the kitchen or the bedroom. She put food and water for the cat near the kitchen door while muttering, "The house is mine and the garden is yours, that should do for you." She'd gotten used to talking to herself since her husband had been abducted and disappeared. When Sabah went out into the garden, it was just after one in the morning, but the light of the full moon illuminated a spot shaded by old trees, casting what seemed to be one big beam of late-day sun broken by the shadows of their branches on the ground. She sat on a chair under the Acadinia tree, whose branches were leaning away from the direction of the sea, and lit a cigarette. The wrinkles on her face appeared as thin dark lines drawn on an area of light on her crystal, white skin, surrounded by her abundant, dyed hair. Anyone who saw her could easily discern that she was beautiful despite her obvious obesity and the sway of her body, which in its curves had surpassed the beauty standards of the time. Hers was a beauty that passes by without a big fuss, without digging deeply into the memories of those who see it. Her body's curves weren't the era's big news, but she brought them with her from her Turkish adolescence in Mardin.

Sabah turned her head backward after the pain had subsided a bit. She felt terrible regret that she had allowed that woman, Maya, to open up an old wound she thought she'd healed. Why did Sabah tell her what she'd told her? She didn't know how all this had happened. It was as if a fountain inside her exploded as soon as the visitor sat down beside her. She started talking and didn't stop until the woman stood up to leave because she would be late in picking up her young son from daycare.

A stray dog's barking could be heard moving from place to place, while Sabah was sitting on her chair in the garden, at night, muttering. She blamed, in fact cursed, herself, thinking that she was endlessly stupid! She stood up and walked toward the corner of the garden, which overlooked downtown Beirut. She leaned her body against the rusty fence that on one side ran along the walls of Bashoura Cemetery, which was within view of her house. "A stone's throw away," the residents of the buildings around Bashoura said and then added, "Death here's just a stone's throw away." Sabah always stopped at this corner to look for a better place than this sprawling land, full of marble headstones. She was always searching for the most decent place for Ahmad, who was both her cousin and husband—a place that she could see from this corner of the garden when she was standing, leaning on the fence. She thought that if they had returned him to her, even dead, she would have buried him over there on the eastern side, which got the morning sunlight. She'd have been able to visit him with her Auntie Fawziya every Friday, putting flowers on his grave and talking to him. But as it was, Sabah couldn't do even this small thing; she didn't even know if he was alive or dead. She could see a bit of the sea from the southern side. It wasn't very far away, but she visited it rarely; she used to do so with women from the neighborhood before they emigrated during the war years and scattered throughout all of God's world. They used to go down to the sea every year on the last Wednesday in April, to celebrate Job's Wednesday.

They would take off their stockings and walk on water like prophetesses.

In front of her, Sabah could see the destroyed city center, which had remained dark all through the war years, lit up back then only when rockets crossed the sky. Today it was lit up by giant fog lights, under which bulldozers were hard at work, throwing everything they could find into that same sea which swallowed up the stories and memories of the living as well as the dead.

In the area between downtown Beirut and the streets of the lower part of the neighborhood where she lived, the bulldozers had started demolishing the rubble left by the war. People who were living in apartments that weren't theirs were told to leave, to allow for the reconstruction of downtown.

Sabah went back to her chair in the garden, lit another cigarette, and wondered at how this woman had come into her home and gotten her to talk. She hadn't told anyone her life's secrets, which she'd carried with her since she was a twelve-year-old girl, secrets about her life either in Mardin or in Beirut. But when Maya arrived, everything she'd tried to hide came rushing back to her. There was a knock at the door, Sabah looked out the little kitchen window and saw a thin, short, woman in her forties, brown hair covering half her face. She opened the door to her with the one sentence she usually repeated on the tip of her tongue: "You have the wrong address!" But as soon as she opened the door, before she could say anything, the visitor announced:

"I'm looking for someone called Sabah." She said this with seeming exhaustion.

The woman didn't have the address wrong. *She means me*, thought Sabah. For a moment, Sabah wanted to say, "There's no one here by that name," but somehow the idea that a completely unknown woman she'd never seen before had come to visit her warmed her heart. The fact that she'd meant her specifically, her and no one else. *Does she have some updated news about my husband? Is she from the Red Cross? Or a journalist who wants to remind people of us and then will forget us once again? Did she come because of something to do with the mass graves in different Beirut neighborhoods for the missing and murdered? If so, why now? Why me? How did she find me, when the face of the neighborhood changed so much during the war that no one even knew the address of their own house, let alone anyone else's?*

A continual stream of questions ran through Sabah's mind before she responded, "Yes, that's me. I'm Sabah, and who are you?"

"I'm Maya Amer. I'm making a film about downtown Beirut. I wanted to meet people who were living in this area before and during the war. They told me that you never left, you stayed here for more than twenty-five years."

"Come in," Sabah told her, but before she had permission, Maya had already stepped in, passing by Sabah and walking toward the living room. Maya was short and fragile: you could see the delicate bones of her back through her tight black shirt, which was hanging down over her full, dark skirt. Her body tottered under the weight of the black leather handbag hanging from her shoulder. She was also carrying a second thick, canvas bag with a camera and other things in it.

They sat down near each other on an long, worn sofa whose ripped cushions Sabah had covered with a piece of colorful fabric she'd brought with her from Mardin.

Maya opened her bag and took out newspaper articles, papers, photos, and a little notebook covered in writing in various languages. She placed it in a pile on her lap, where it rested for some time, as if it were a small child. Then she spoke: "I've been photographing abandoned, semidestroyed, deserted buildings. In one of the flats, I found a suitcase full of letters, photos, diaries, old newspapers, and so on. I found your name and address on a big envelope that had documents and other things in it—folded up papers, a phone directory of businesses downtown that are no longer there, and old photographs, some of which have your name written on the back. They are definitely photos of you. That's how I found you. The mukhtar who owns the grocery store at the top of the street told me where your place was."

When Maya went into the store to ask the muktar about Sabah Karbouz and an address she wasn't sure of, she wasn't expecting to find the answer so easily. The seventy-something mukhtar got up from his wooden chair, putting his hand on his heart to apologize for not shaking Maya's hand, which she had held out to greet him. A woman who was standing in the shop smiled, telling Maya, "The Hajj doesn't shake women's hands." Meanwhile, the mukhtar walked in front of her to the shop entrance, pointing out the blocked road at the bottom of the bigger street.

He seemed surprised at Maya's question about Sabah. "Be wary of her, she's a bit loony, and she has seizures. Everyone knows her here. She's as old as bread.... Ha ha ha!" He laughed ridiculously while Maya said good-bye and gave a wave of her hand, as if to say, "Don't worry, I'll find it." Then she hurried off in the direction of the alley he had indicated.

**

Maya had found the suitcase of photos and papers in Ibrahim's flat. He was the Jewish man who left Beirut and emigrated during the war, Sabah thought while lighting her third cigarette. She had brought her personal possessions with her when she moved into his place. She worked for him as a maid; she'd heard his sobs when his wife died. When she started getting really busy working in the little kiosk she'd rented, she transferred the responsibility of looking after Ibrahim and his apartment to her friend Mariam. But she kept on visiting him. Then, suddenly, he'd emigrated to Israel without her knowing. He told her that he was going to visit his son in America for a month and then come back. He lied to everyone including her, whom he trusted and who trusted him. Then all the remaining Jews in Beirut emigrated. Since the beginning of the war they'd been under the protection of Yasser Arafat, who distinguished between Israelis and Jews. However, Israel's invasion and occupation of Lebanon all the way to Beirut forced Arafat to leave Lebanon by sea, headed for Tunis aboard a Greek ship. Like him, all the remaining Jews emigrated—mostly to Israel, Europe, and America.

Arafat left Beirut destroyed and broken. But despite this, the last words he delivered at the city's coastline were, "Glory itself should kneel down before you, Beirut!" From that time on, though, glory didn't kneel down even once before Beirut, indeed Beirut knelt down, insulted and humiliated—and not at the hands of the Israeli army alone but also the Syrian mukhabarat, the Syrian army, and the many different Lebanese militias.

After a time, Sabah was forced to stop frequenting Ibrahim's place. It became dangerous to stay too long at his house at the bottom of Zuqaq al-Blat, across from Riad El Solh Square. Despite the total lack of safety in the area, Ibrahim's building and those around it were quickly occupied by families who had come from areas controlled by Christian militias or were fleeing from more dangerous areas in the South. Some of their family members were fighters and belonged to militias. Many people also came from Nebaa, Karantina, and Bourj Hammoud to the Khandaq al-Ghamiq building. The first newly arrived families lived in the Armenian doctor's house, then another family in the flat across from it. The face of the neighborhood changed, as did the faces of its residents. Sabah no longer knew any of them. The new families came, carrying their possessions, their furniture, and their stories. Their stories were mixed with those of the people who left, and with time Sabah could no longer distinguish between them.

Sabah lived throughout the war years in her old apartment, not far from the square downtown where there was constant fighting. She lived as if she were on another planet, and her flat was safe thanks to Bashoura Cemetery, which witnessed the wars in downtown Beirut. From afar the cemetery looked like a hill that was a comma separating the fighters—as if death alone were separating the enemies, death and its vigilant shadows. "The walls of the house of death protect us from death," Sabah would say. The sandbags blocking the entrance to the narrow street, rising up toward the sky like high walls, gave the street's inhabitants more security. Egyptian workers, then Syrian and South Asian ones, filled the bags and piled them up on top of each other under the watch of the armed men of the neighborhood and the butts of their rifles. A massive sandbag blockade was erected on the eastern side of the neighborhood. Over there, people started moving along another route; instead of all four directions, people's lives were limited to only two.

Many papers remained in Ibrahim's house when Sabah left. Personal papers and photos and old tickets and an expired travel document belonging to Ahmad Karbouz. She'd left that all behind; she'd also left behind Noura's envelopes, papers, diaries and things that had belonged to Noura's child.

The bombardment never reached the Khandaq al-Ghamiq building directly during the war, and Sabah stayed on with the few residents who remained on their street bordered by Bashoura on one side and running along the edge of downtown. They would hear the sounds of the war very near them, the three-story building would shake and they would feel like it was going to crash down on their heads. The building's garden, which had become an extension of Sabah's apartment, was home to acacia, pomegranate, and fig trees, as well as Acadinias—all of which themselves had heard the sounds of violence from nearby. The apartment residents had left the building and scattered; some of them moved to their villages and stayed there, while others found apartments in different Beirut neighborhoods. Everyone was seeking safety and to be far from death. Some left Lebanon never to return. Those who owned the apartments tried to sell them before emigrating as far as America. The neighborhood seemed to have suddenly aged all in one shot. Sandbags were put in place, so some of the streets led to nowhere.

When it rained, the closed-off, lower streets transformed into little lakes the neighborhood children went out to play and splash their feet in, even though their homes still had no running water.

When the war began, Sabah had just started adding a bedroom and kitchen to the little caretaker's room she and her husband lived in. She drew measurements on the garden floor, using white chalk to mark the place for the doors, window, sink, and another door leading out to the garden. She started doing all this with the help of a Sudanese laborer who brought her bricks that he piled up high, then climbed the stairs, lining up a row of stones after first putting down cement mixed with sand and water. The new bedroom and kitchen walls looked somewhat strange from the garden side, when compared to the crumbling old walls of this building and others nearby. However, the forces of nature and years of war soon made it a part of the neighborhood scene. Sabah managed her life on this narrow street; by candlelight she balanced the accounts of the little kiosk she'd rented since 1979. Listening to the continuous sounds of death and the daily news about the kidnappings of many young men in the neighborhood and surrounding areas pained her. These men went out and never returned; no one knew anything about their fate, but that pain itself made her stronger—beginning with the kidnapping of her own young husband at the beginning of 1976, only two days after New Year's Eve. He insisted on going to the east side of the divided Beirut to return to work in the restaurant, which had moved there. He never arrived. The continual sense of loss made Sabah's desire to live flourish despite everything, a talisman of sorts to help ensure her survival. She'd lost her boyfriend, Ahmad, who abandoned her when he emigrated alone. And now here she was losing the second Ahmad, who was her husband. Nothing tied the two Ahmads in her heart except their name. Her sadness filled her womb like a dead baby. She swallowed it like the sea swallows up the corpses of the disappeared. "That's life," Sabah would say to Noura Abu Sawwan, expressing her discontent in this way to the Syrian journalist who had come to Beirut and settled there two or three years after Sabah had, or to the women of the homes she'd work in, repeating, "Yes … my life is just leaving and loss."

8
MARDIN / BEIRUT

Maya spread the photos on the table and scrutinized each one with Sabah. "Yes, these are pictures of me. Here I am by myself in front of our house in Mardin, my village in Turkey. I haven't visited in years. This one is with my husband Ahmad, who paid to get out of his Turkish military service, but poor thing was kidnapped in Beirut and I've had no news of him since."

From time to time, Sabah stopped speaking, hesitating for a moment. She was silent whenever Maya looked for another photo. Her husband, Ahmad Karbouz, had disappeared at the beginning of the war. Seven years earlier, they'd been married by a shaykh and she'd come with him from Mardin to Beirut in 1969. She'd always wanted to collect the photos in a family album. But she kept putting it off and never actually bought an album. When her husband was kidnapped, she felt there was no need for the album anymore. She lost the family photos the day she left Khawaja Ibrahim's home. When she returned to her own home she brought two photos of the kidnapped Ahmad with her and she left everything else of hers and Noura's in a suitcase in the attic, where Maya had found it. One year passed, then another, and another, and Sabah met other women whose men had been kidnapped. She started bringing a picture of her missing husband with her to gatherings of the families of the disappeared, hanging it on her chest among muffled cries and weeping, standing there for a long time before finally returning home. She froze whenever she found herself amid flashing cameras, watching the women who'd organized these demonstrations, women who could look right into the cameras and talk. Sabah couldn't hear what they were saying. She would stand and look around, as if searching for someone. She would always feel strange in those moments. *I'll stay a stranger and he'll stay my kidnapped man, I'm the only one who misses him,* she would tell herself, going home after removing the picture from her chest and putting it back into her handbag.

Sabah hung the other picture of her missing husband on her bedroom wall and started talking to it at night when she was in bed to cut through her fear of being alone. She'd gotten used to him in the seven years that they'd lived together. She wasn't passionately in love with him but felt close to him and had become his friend. Every night, when he came back from working in the restaurant, he'd take what he'd earned out of his pocket and hand it to her. He told her he wanted to buy her a house, better than the one she dreamed of when she ran away with her boyfriend Ahmad. He would always say that he couldn't give her children because of an illness he had as a boy that left him sterile, but he could buy her a house. So she hid the money inside the white cotton stuffing of her pillows, saying that banks weren't safe. After the failure of Intrabank and what had happened to her Auntie Fawziya, who'd lost the money she'd had there, Sabah wouldn't trust any bank. She started relying on the small amount she earned by working and that her husband made as their building's caretaker. The domestic work Sabah did for people in the building made them overlook the fact that Ahmad was away every evening, working in a restaurant where he washed dishes and cleaned up before closing. When the war started, the restaurant closed down and its owner moved to East Beirut, where he opened up another restaurant.

After her husband was abducted, each week Sabah took out one little pile of the money hidden inside her pillow, to pay off "the good boys." They would knock on her door and come in, promising to bring her husband back safely. They'd seen him and spoken to him, he was still alive, and he'd sent her a verbal message asking her to give the "good boys" what they asked for. They came and went with new news and new requests for things the kidnapped men wanted.

Sabah didn't know how she ran out of all the liras she'd hidden to buy a house. She never lost hope even though she totally ran out of money. She didn't stop looking for domestic work, though she was also working every day in the kiosk. But the people in the neighborhood changed, and the new residents didn't pay people to work in their houses. She kept waiting for the "good boys," who never returned after she'd told them that she didn't have any more money. Sometimes, sitting in bed in the evenings, she started feeling like Ahmad's shadow was moving around his picture. She started complaining, but he kept silent. She admonished him, crying, and then when she was exhausted from crying, she'd turn her head around and sleep as though they were quarrelling.

The day after he disappeared they told her he'd come back in two days. She cleaned the house, changed the sheets, and waited, and then she waited more. Some time passed before the horrible question, which she could not bear, crossed her mind: *What if he never returns?*

Sabah stopped talking while Maya kept looking at the pictures. Silence fell over the two of them, and during those moments, time passed slowly and heavily.

"That was a long time ago," Sabah said, as though apologizing for her silence, while looking at a black-and-white photograph of her with her parents and auntie, standing in front of the house in Mardin. In the picture, she was wearing a long dress with flowers at the chest and waist. Her auntie had brought it from Beirut so that the fourteen-year-old girl could wear it on her wedding day. She also brought her white high-heel shoes, but they were too big and Sabah had to stuff them with paper so they would fit. Her auntie started arranging the dress on the bride's chest, telling her proudly that she'd bought it from Mouadeb's, the Jewish shop in Souq Ayyas, and that Sabah couldn't find a more beautiful one in all of Beirut. The picture was taken the day she left Turkey for Lebanon. First she took a small bus and then a much larger one, a sort she'd never taken before. She was on the road for more than two days before she arrived in Beirut. Her father married her off quickly so people would stop talking about her and the family's honor. The gossip continued for months. She didn't know how long it had been since she'd looked at these pictures of herself, which were enough to bring back a past that she'd reckoned was buried forever, never to return. But it had returned.

She remembered ... and yet the memory came tenuously, incomplete.

That day her dress was pink, Sabah said.

Her eyes grew moist and she laughed.

Sabah hadn't yet reached the age of fourteen when her Auntie Fawziya came at the end of spring from Beirut to Mardin. Her father had sent for her auntie, accompanied by her son, Ahmad, to ask for his daughter's hand. At the beginning of the year, Sabah had run off with the brother of one of her female relatives by marriage. They'd exchanged kisses behind the nearby cemetery and then lain down together in an embrace and she'd gotten dry grass in her hair and clothes. She loved him and saw him in her dreams. He promised her they'd travel abroad together to Germany where his sister was. She also dreamed of travelling to this new country. He said, "Life is better there, we'll be able to do anything." On that one damp day at the end of winter, she'd ridden behind him on his motorbike through the narrow roads. They were both happy.

At first they didn't know where they were going. He wanted to take her to his family's house in Diyarbakir to finish getting ready for the trip, but they refused to let them in, fearing Sabah's family, and the trouble it would no doubt create between her mother and the women of his family.

Her father then asked the boyfriend she'd eloped with to bring her back home under the threat of imprisonment, because Sabah was still a minor. Turkish law did not allow underage marriage. Her father was also afraid of being punished should he agree to her marriage. The father, as well as the husband could be sanctioned for signing the marriage contract of an underage girl. But despite this fear, such marriages were often conducted secretly, in religious ceremonies, and then when a bride reached legal age they would be registered officially.

And so the fear Sabah's father felt stemmed not from his opposing underage marriage; he himself had married his wife when she was less than thirteen, in a religious ceremony, as happened frequently back then. Only more than five years later did he register the marriage with the authorities.

No marriage means no trip to Germany for me, Sabah thought. *It also means I won't get a visa, because what would my role be if I travelled with my boyfriend Ahmad?* Sabah lamented, but quickly forgot about it, consoling herself by thinking that she'd just spent twenty days roaming around Turkish villages and cities she'd never visited in her whole life. To get to Istanbul they'd spent more than a full day and night in a big bus before arriving. Ahmad took his motorbike out of the bus's back door with the help of another passenger, not reacting to the cursing of the driver, who wasn't satisfied with the sum he'd received for the favor. They were hosted by a friend living in the Eyup neighborhood whom her boyfriend knew from his military service. Sabah wasn't relaxed around him or his mother, who treated her as though she were a streetwalker.

She tried to avoid the young man's eyes whenever she walked in front of him to go to the bathroom near the kitchen. The two of them spent four days in the city that never sleeps, and Sabah didn't sleep, either, not even for one minute. She sat up awake, counting the cars passing by, whose lights were reflected in the mirror on the wardrobe, while listening to the sounds of Ahmad deep in sleep. She wondered how he could sleep in a city like Istanbul. She wanted to go out instead of sleeping, she wanted to walk through those streets so full of lights. She didn't want to go back to the village; she was tense and afraid.

When Ahmad told her it would be impossible for him to get her a visa, Sabah started crying bitterly, as if she'd lost her dream of a lifetime. She remembered that he didn't try to console her but instead told her she was stupid, that living abroad wouldn't be paradise but actually difficult and arduous. That night, as she sat and watched the cars passing by, she shook him while he was sleeping near her, telling him that it would be all right—let paradise be here and not in Germany. "Istanbul is beautiful," she said. "Let's stay here instead of travelling! We can find a room, a room in a building on Istiklal Street! We'll find work for sure." She'd started to imagine a simple, good life with Ahmad. But he didn't hear her, he didn't listen to what she was saying, and he changed all their plans after calling Mardin a couple of times. In the few days they spent in Istanbul, Sabah furnished a house for the two of them in her imagination: it had a bed, a sofa, a wardrobe, a refrigerator, a gas stove, and a red rug. She even imagined the plants she would grow by the entrance and saw them growing, flowering, blooming. However, Ahmad suddenly resolved to take her back to her family. Sabah didn't understand what seemed to her a crazy decision. He remained silent and didn't inform her about the content of the last telephone call he had with Mardin. In the morning Sabah was sad and didn't feel like eating the now-cold, kefta sandwich she'd bought the day before—which by now was just a stale leftover, like their dreams.

She sat behind him on the motorbike and held onto him, feeling at that moment that he no longer cared if she were encircling his waist from behind with her arms or resting her head on his shoulders. He didn't turn around and lean his head toward her face as he had done before. He sped up and she begged him to slow down, for fear of falling off, but he didn't respond; in fact he increased his speed. He seemed angry with her.

Sabah went back home twenty days after she and Ahmad left, and from that time on she heard everyone talking about her as if she were guilt itself, saying that she was "madqoura," meaning someone had touched her, and that no man would ever agree to marry her. She didn't understand what this meant—"someone had touched her"—and she started imagining that she had been stricken with an illness, perhaps an infectious disease transmitted through touching, one she might now pass on to others if she so much as spoke, laughed, or even smiled. She imagined that no one should touch her anymore. Her mother refused to greet her, and so did her father. "Get inside, Sabah," he said to her, harshly, looking into her mother's eyes instead of at her, searching for his daughter in her mother's face. That night she couldn't escape a severe beating by her father. Her voice rang out through the neighborhood, carrying above the cypress trees surrounding the cemetery. No doubt everyone heard the sound of her screams and cries. Surely death too had heard them and had come, since her grandmother, who had given her name to her, passed away that very night. Word had it that she couldn't bear her granddaughter's return: "If only she'd been the one to go, instead of her grandmother." It was also said that she died because she couldn't stand her name being so defiled.

Sabah knew that she had left with Ahmad against everyone's wishes. She also knew that the small period of time she'd spent out of the house had comprised the most wonderful days of her life, and that if she could do it again, she would, without any hesitation—even if she died from her father's beating. She returned, but she didn't return as the person she had been. She used to be Sabah and she came back another Sabah. That was how everyone saw her. *So I've became "madqoura,"* Sabah thought. Maybe that's why her father sent for his sister, who lived in Beirut, to come and ask for her hand in marriage to her son, who was five years older than Sabah. He wasn't yet twenty. His name was also Ahmad. Sabah thought this would be easier, him having the same name as her boyfriend who'd brought her back to her family's house and disappeared. She heard her uncle's wife say that his family had disowned him and he'd gone to Germany. He went where his sister had emigrated but didn't take Sabah with him as he'd promised.

Without meaning to, Sabah started calling all young men "Ahmad," even her brother Moheiddine. As soon as he heard the name Ahmad, he knocked the wind out of her with a slap across the face, drawing blood from her teeth. Wearing his football shoes, he kicked her all over her stomach and chest. She protected her head with her hands, crying on the ground, curled up like a ball he loved kicking. Their father said nothing to his son and instead smiled at him, almost congratulating him. In her father's eyes, Sabah's younger brother had become a man the moment he kicked her.

Sabah cried when she saw the picture Maya handed to her. Maya thought that despite the years that had passed, longing made Sabah cry and still pained her. But Sabah was crying for reasons Maya couldn't understand or even guess. She cried for Mardin, her childhood, and her sick mother, for lost love and loneliness that had driven her to the edge of madness. She cried for her missing man, whom she didn't love but had gotten used to living with. Maya didn't feel all this—how could she?

Maya wanted to ask Sabah about the letters, the child she was carrying in one of the photos, and her disappeared husband. She wanted to ask her about Noura: about Noura's diaries and who she was, and about Kemal and his letters that had found their way into Maya's heart, as if they'd been addressed to her. But she didn't, and instead left Sabah to carry on with her story.

**

"But how do I know if I'll like Ahmad, Auntie Fawziya's son?" Sabah asked her father after she'd been convinced that marriage was inevitable, and after she'd already started dreaming of Beirut instead of Germany or Istanbul. "Is your nephew tall, broad shouldered, and handsome?" she asked, because she hadn't seen him since she'd been a little girl. Her father didn't respond but, talking to himself, said things that made her hate him even more: "Someone like her can't start putting conditions on her marriage." "This is a family issue," said her mother, stealing the conversation from her father while looking at Sabah with harsh eyes. She added cynically, not without blame, "After what you did, your cousin had a duty to cover it up and marry you, but it turned out he had no family pride, for he disappeared." She seemed to be directing what she was saying at Sabah, but in reality she wanted Sabah's father to hear it even more—that the person with "no family pride" was her husband's brother's son. Indeed, this was a golden opportunity for Sabah's mother to preempt any accusation of her being the mother of a "madqoura" girl. To retaliate, she therefore laid the blame on her husband's entire family.

The auntie soon arrived with her silent, shy son, who was infertile because of a childhood paralysis, which afflicted his left leg. She came and asked for Sabah's hand in marriage to protect her reputation, because the girl's reputation was the same as her auntie's, as the mother said the moment her husband's sister arrived from Beirut. "The reputation of all the women in the family is so interconnected!" Sabah thought as she threw her body on her bed and slept.

Her father wanted to marry her off to stop the gossip, but at the same time he wanted to get her dowry, which he'd set at 2,000 Lebanese lira, enough in those days to buy himself a used car. Her auntie would have to pay the dowry before the shaykh would draw up a marriage contract between Sabah and her son. The aunt told her brother, directly, with total insolence, as she opened her handbag and took out a stack of banknotes, "I have 500 lira, that's it. Either you take it and be grateful, or I'll go back to Beirut with my son. You should thank God that I am taking your daughter off your hands." She threw the pile of notes on the little table between them and continued, "No one except me would take her, and a thousand girls are hoping for my son. You're the one who should be paying, not me!" Sabah's mother then intervened, shouting at Fawziya, "Don't act like such a goody-goody! The girl's just like you. You ran off with your husband twenty-two years ago. What, have you forgotten? 'Girls take after their fathers' sisters,' as they say, and don't forget the state your son is in, he can barely walk!"

Sabah heard everything while standing near the door of the room, looking at the banknotes spread all over the table.

What a shameless auntie, Sabah thought. *How can my father put up with her? How can he not kick her out of the house? But he wants me to marry her son and travel to Beirut so she'll cover everything up. As if Beirut were a drapery for the family, a landfill for its squandered honour.*

Sabah walked outside and saw her cousin Ahmad sitting on a wooden chair in front of the house, his head twisted on his shoulder as if he were sleeping, his eyelids quivering in the sunshine. He looked like the village idiot she used to wander around with, like other girls her age. She felt a sudden tenderness toward him and thought that the two of them—she and him—in a way were similar. She went back into the room, the noise of the family's fighting still filling the air, and she shrank into the mattress laid out on the ground. She put her hands over her ears. She didn't want to hear any more. She didn't want to see: she'd heard and seen a lot.

The morning of the next day, Sabah looked out the window of the little room and saw her Auntie Fawziya going up the stairs leading to the cemetery only about 200 meters from the house. Sabah's grandmother—Fawziya's mother—was buried there. This was the first time Fawziya had visited since her mother died. She had come not only to ask for Sabah's hand but also to visit her mother's grave. Sabah's grandmother had died months ago, and Fawziya hadn't come at the time. They said that she didn't come so as not to be burdened by her brother's "madqoura" daughter—the one no one would marry after she came back home from her less than three-week journey on a motorbike with her boyfriend. Fawziya stood in front of the tomb. She cried, beat her chest, and wailed for her mother. No one in the family cried over the grandmother on the day she died, and everyone felt really annoyed by the visiting woman's gravesite mourning, because it reminded them that they themselves had shed not a single tear during the funeral, and they weren't able to cry now and participate in her daughter's belated mourning. Her mother's death hadn't been enough for Fawziya to come for the burial, to pay the cost of a ticket from Beirut to Mardin. She had waited until she was coming for more than one reason: once she'd agreed to marry Sabah to her son, she could mourn her mother and marry her son off at the same time.

When Sabah ran away with Ahmad, her mother stood in front of the door to the house and told her son Moheiddine, looking straight into his eyes, "Go bring your sister back, and don't touch a hair on her head. She's my daughter and I will deal with her. If you hurt her I will strangle you with my own two hands." Their mother's voice rang out, her eyes shining. Her anger always used to scare Sabah and Moheiddine alike.

As for their father, he put his head in his hands and cried like a baby.

Riding behind Ahmad on his motorbike, Sabah felt like she owned the entire world. Ahmad turned the throttle, the engine revved up, and he took off. Sabah's long brown hair flew behind her, and she no longer cared about anyone in her family. She didn't think about her father or brother. This moment made her feel that she could abandon the whole world. Just then she didn't know what she loved more: Ahmad or the sensation of flying!

When she was in Istanbul, Sabah saw many lovers strolling near the Galata Bridge. She loved looking at the couples when they were holding each other close. Doing so soothed her spirits. She looked at them once when walking next to Ahmad and found herself taking his hand and lifting it to her face. She did this with a little sigh. He looked at her and seemed to disapprove. His look alone made her tense, and her feelings changed. Instead of kissing his hand she found herself pressing her teeth into it and biting down with all her strength. Ahmad started shouting and pushed her backward so she almost fell, grabbing his wounded hand with the other one. He cursed her in a choppy voice while rubbing his hand.

She didn't know why she bit him. Perhaps she was angry. He told her she was insane and not at all like other women.

9
SABAH: FORGOTTEN MEMORIES

Sabah carried on narrating bits of her life story, and Maya handed her a black-and-white photograph. She took it, stood up, and walked from the sofa to the narrow window so she could see the photo more clearly in the light of the sun. It was a picture of a woman carrying a small child in her arms.

"Ah ... That's me about sixteen years ago!"

The picture showed her wearing a long, dark gray dress with wide sleeves, carrying a small child whose face looked older than his age.

"My God, that's me, and the child is Noura's son. A woman called Adèle al-Naa'es took our picture." Sabah thought that this child's story had ended just as the war had ended. But the story came back to her when this thin woman entered her house.

Sabah was muttering in a shaky voice, as Maya came close to her to ask her who the child was. It was as if in that moment Maya had transported her to a time she would prefer to forget.

"Small child? My God, what could I possibly want from a past that comes raging back to me like a wild beast ...?" She asked in a choked-up, sobbing voice.

Sabah grew silent, trying to regain her composure, and then said, "He and his mother died in an explosion. They were killed. Oh, that was a long time ago. I forgot. I've forgotten everything. I can't remember anything at all."

Silence overtook them and they both sunk in thoughts that were difficult to share. *It's as if I've opened up the floodgates of Sabah's memory,* Maya thought. *Everyone is trying to forget here, or trying to select what they want to remember, Sabah isn't the only one. Sometimes it happens that we start imagining that we no longer have anything but forgetfulness, but it's an illusion, since memory rises up again like a phoenix, infuses life into the veins of our soul, and returns us to reality.*

Maya thought all this to herself silently. Sabah meanwhile became conscious of the fact that she was telling a story she'd previously decided to forget and never come back to—to erase what was recorded in her memory. The choice of her remembering fleeing from her house as a teenaged girl, a child really, wasn't a coincidence. Neither was the choice of the memory of Mardin, Istanbul, her marriage, and her trip to Beirut. Those chosen memories were fine, but it was more difficult to return to a memory whose violent history was closer to the present.

Suddenly Sabah stood up and asked Maya, in an emphatic, anxiety-filled voice, "You, what do you do exactly? I didn't understand? Why are you here? You said you were working? On what? Where?"

"I'm shooting a film, as I told you … part of the project of reconstructing Beirut."

"Reconstructing, reconstruction," Sabah replied. "Every day on radio and television they talk like this, too. Maybe they want to build and construct so that people will forget. They said they would pile up the stones of the demolished buildings in the sea, but where will they pile up the stench of blood and decay? The blood I saw down below, and here, and there. I saw it flowing every day, the blood of every nationality, every sect. Blood from every building. Ahmad's blood will be piled up there, too." Sabah choked up a bit and continued, pointing her hand at her chest. "Sure, blood can dry up, but what will I do with the dark blood stain that remains here in my heart? Why did Ahmad disappear? Why did those who died, die? Why did Noura die? Look there and see!"

Sabah carried on, pointing out the window at downtown Beirut: "Look how Beirut is being reconstructed after it was demolished! The people who destroyed it are still there; they haven't left. They're in parliament, they run the government. Nothing's been resolved!"

Sabah was silent, as if a huge amount of anger had left her and disappeared. She wanted to be silent now because she couldn't understand how her story had escaped her, and because she didn't know what to do with this leftover emptiness now that her anger had come out. Maya also remained silent. The sounds of children in the alley rose up and entered the building. Their shouting was mixed with the banging of a ball against the ground and the old building's façade. Maya gathered the pictures that were spread all over the table, and asked Sabah for a glass of water.

Sabah went into the kitchen, and soon the scent of cardamom-flavored coffee spread all through the house and mixed into the air in the little sitting room.

Sabah's voice rang out again, continuing her story, as she put a tray with the hot pot of coffee, cups, some sweets, and a glass of water in front of Maya.

Ever since arriving in Beirut in 1969, Sabah had witnessed the changes that occurred in the neighborhood, starting with the building she lived in and then later the other buildings around it.

The Armenian doctor who lived on the first floor was the first to leave the building. In 1975, he left with his wife, who had been born into an Armenian family in Aleppo and never got used to living in Beirut. That's what she told her neighbors, and Sabah heard echoes of her story while working in her and the doctor's apartment. He was a well-known medical doctor who wouldn't take a single lira from her when he treated her. He took care of her and gave her medicines for free. Once Sabah insisted on going up to help out his wife, and worked in their apartment for a whole day. She cleaned the rugs and chandeliers and washed all the winter blankets and bed covers. She explained that this was to repay the doctor's kindness and generosity. This couple emigrated to California, where the wife's family was. Her family there bought her and her husband enormous vineyards in the valley, not far from Los Angeles, and they started making red and white wine to sell all over the United States.

At the start of her new life in Beirut, Sabah worked with her auntie sewing colored beads onto the ready-made fabric of abayas and dresses for weddings and parties that Fawziya got from the owners of the Mouadeb shop in Souq Ayyas. The Jewish shop owner supplied her with the necessary materials: beads, rolls of quality cloth, and thread. Her auntie hired young Kurdish women from the neighborhood to work for her, sewing beads onto party dresses. Then she'd return to the owner of the bead shop days before the delivery date to take more. But when the Mouadeb family left, as had all the other Jewish families before them, the final materials remained in Fawziya's possession; she didn't deliver them to a merchant and she didn't pay the workers their salaries, as she couldn't sell them. They stayed in her cupboard for years before she was able to sell them off to an elderly woman who sewed abayas for women from the Gulf for the little cash that she could get.

Since the bulldozers had started the reconstruction, Sabah hadn't set foot downtown. "There's nothing for us down there," she had said to her women neighbors, who were hesitating between going down and watching from their ancient balconies, which looked to someone from outside as though they might fall off the outer walls of the apartments right into the gardens below. "What's there for us?" Sabah asked, adding, "When I think about going down, my skin crawls. I don't want to!"

Sabah didn't want to talk a lot—either about the child, or his mother, Noura Abu Sawwan. She didn't answer Maya's many questions about this photo, as if she wanted to forget.

Maya stopped asking questions and told Sabah that she would come back soon to finish their conversation. She had to pick up her son from daycare. She also wanted to read Noura's diaries, which she'd only flipped through quickly. A huge curiosity about Noura overwhelmed Maya, especially after reading the last letters from Kemal Firat.

10
NOURA'S DIARIES

I've dreamed of being a writer since I was a young girl, and I see newspaper articles as the pinnacle of writing.

The word I was searching for was always on the tip of my tongue, near my heart. But it didn't find itself on paper. It wasn't able to become a material reality in a body with a voice, a rhyme, a rhythm, or an impact. I used to believe that I was afflicted by something, an illness or a lack of power; this affliction put me in an inferior position to other people my age. I remember those other girls in my class. Their laughter used to ring out behind classroom walls and in the playground. I used to walk and laugh with them, when we went down the stairs into the big playground, but just as quickly I would get bored and revert into my far-away solitude. I used to be anxious that I was like this. Then I started to hear stories of their marriages, the children they had, and how they stayed at home.

Time passed before I knew what was up with me, that it was something good that I should look after—a distinction, not an illness.

In Syria, after I decided to come and live in Lebanon, I burned all the thick notebooks I'd filled. At the time, I didn't understand the real reason I'd thrown everything I wrote into the fireplace and then stood near it, looking at the fire consuming the pages and my heart at the same time. Why did I burn everything I'd written? Was I punishing myself for my sister's death or did I want to exorcize my guilt? Or perhaps I burned what I'd written to begin a new life in Beirut, so as not to die in my grandfather's house. My sister Henaa didn't run away, instead she left a letter telling the story of her death.

The first thing I did when I arrived in Beirut was to write down my sister Henaa's story. At the time I didn't know that the pages would also determine my entire life. I wrote the story down, and while writing many things came out into the open. My sister's story changed me. Not only did my sister die, but indeed the old Noura died, too. Now I think that burning everything I'd written was a little suicide, but it was also protecting me, so I couldn't write down my final death. Writing about death was a way to survive. I could understand at the time why my father remained silent, why my cousin Huda ignored what I told her, and why my half-brother decided to remain neutral. The end of my sister Henaa's story was the beginning of mine. However, writing down my sister's story didn't cure me of the desire to settle accounts, which was both my right and that of my sister, who lost her life.

My sister wasn't the only one who drank poisonous pesticides and went to sleep on the floor of the bakeh, where they didn't find her until early evening. No, she wasn't the only one of the women in the family who committed suicide or tried to kill herself. Twenty years before my sister's incident, one of my father's sisters tried in the same way, in a different place. She beat death in the final moments, however.

Many stories about the women in the family—both close and distant relatives—contain the experience of suicide attempts, but most of those women survived. Women retaliate against oppression by oppressing themselves. They are locked in this cycle. If a woman could have understood why she was considering killing herself, she might have been able to stop. Many women refuse to oppress themselves without being able to specify the source of oppression. Despite this, they search for some light of day, they distance themselves, migrate, survive. Is it differences in personality? Or is it different levels of the survival instinct that play a role in women protecting themselves? Henaa's suicide compelled me to put all of these questions on paper, every time I wanted to write about her death. I didn't find an answer but I found myself propelled by an inner strength to break these vicious cycles. I inherited this strength from my mother's mother, who taught me that life is your right. She managed to stay alive by pure chance —when she hadn't even yet turned six years old, a young man from northern Syria took her from an Armenian refugee camp near Aleppo after witnessing the murder of her family. He was a solider in the Ottoman army and was discharged after taking a bullet wound in his arm, which paralyzed his hand. He brought her to his family and told them, "She will be your little sister."

Shahani was her name before the family that adopted her changed both her name and her religion. The family wanted to preserve her name somehow so she wouldn't forget it, so they found her a strange name. She became Shehla. Sometimes my grandmother remembered her original name, conjured up her language, and started humming Armenian songs that she had carried with her since she was a little girl, songs so mixed through time with the typical Aleppo rhythms of qudud halabiya that she no longer knew how to distinguish between them. I used to listen to her, not understanding anything, and most likely even she no longer understood the meanings of the words she was singing. She'd forgotten her language but she hadn't forgotten Mardin, the village from which she'd been displaced with her family as a child.

Perhaps she had forgotten everything except one day when she'd was seventeen years old and she met my grandfather. This meeting changed her life a second time. He was a young man selling sacks of wheat with his father in the Aleppo souqs when he encountered her in her father's shop. She smiled coquettishly when she saw my grandfather, saying, "We won't buy your wheat. We only eat Jazira wheat." She meant the province of al-Jazira, famous for its wheat cultivation. She liked him and wanted to flirt with him, but didn't know how. She was about to leave and travel to teach in a school in the Hauran Mountains, so she travelled with the two of them to become a schoolteacher in a girls' school belonging to Anglican missionaries. She then became the wife of this young man who was to become my grandfather. She started tending to the orchard near the house, trying to grow pistachios there, and it was under the shadows of those trees that she used to sit on cold Aleppo evenings. She never succeeded in growing them in the mountains. She cultivated more and more vineyards and then started making red wine, which she kept in vats from one year to another.

I didn't know the details of my grandmother's story—the death of her family, her being a refugee in Aleppo—until after my mother's death, when we started visiting her house more often in the mountain village of Rummaneh. It had become our second home, especially after my father remarried. We would spend the entire summer there and only return to Damascus when the school year began. My grandmother's life was a chopped-up story with no past or origin. My mother didn't tell her story or pass it down to us. My mother was silent, as if she had been born from the roots of a tree and not a woman's womb. For my grandmother and me, words only found their way to us one day after my mother's death when I accompanied her to the bakeh and the storage lofts. I watched her cleaning clusters of grapes at the beginning of the autumn, mashing them up and putting them in earthenware vats to ferment them, leaving some of them to dry into raisins, which she would then add to dishes full of boiled wheat along with almonds and walnuts. She sat on the ground and filled large preserving jars with olives. She then added bits of lemon and red pepper, poured salted water over them, and finished off her artistry by layering pure olive oil over the green olives.

On that first autumn after my mother's death, when I hadn't yet turned ten, my grandmother Shahani told me her story. While she told it I was both listening and watching what she was doing. I was like someone hearing two stories at the same time. One was the story of her childhood and adolescence in Aleppo with the family that raised her but that, at the end of the day, wasn't her family. The other was her story of her suffering in adapting to wild, mountainous nature and family relations, both of which were hard.

When Henaa's body was found in the bakeh near the house, my grandmother was at the end of her life. She couldn't get up or walk outside anymore. She started mourning from her bed, saying that there weren't any snakes in the bakeh and that what the family was saying about the cause of Henaa's death was simply foolishness.

The last time I visited her, I said I wanted to travel. She had declined a lot from the time of my previous visit at Eid al-Adha. She'd stopped making wine and visiting the vineyards. She started giving me advice, and repeating that travel was a blessing, that today is life, and that life is a right that shouldn't be postponed until tomorrow—that wherever I am will become the mirror of my soul and no doubt come to resemble me. Shahani, as I always liked to call her, didn't live much longer. She passed on days before the first anniversary of Henaa's passing, two weeks before I left.

**

My grandmother died, and the shaykhs and neighbors in Rumanneh refused to perform the funeral prayers for her. They said that there was no mercy for a woman whose origins at birth were so distant from their sect, and that they would burn in hell if they performed them. All of their stupidity was just because she wasn't a birth member of the sect. My mother's brother insisted on bringing in religious men who were known for being more open minded than those in the village to perform the prayers. After that happened, my uncle changed. He no longer maintained any friendly relations with the families of the shaykhs; he no longer participated in their joys and sorrows. My grandmother's death made him recall a fact that he'd forgotten for some time now but knew previously throughout his life devoted to clandestine, leftist struggles: that death is the perfect opportunity for religious people to take revenge on living people—they punish their dead by closing their path to heaven. When faced with mysterious, incomprehensible things, they accuse living people of renouncing their responsibilities. This is how heaven becomes closed not only to the dead but also to the living.

**

I decided to travel because I wanted to survive. I didn't want either that heaven or that death. I wanted survival first of all, then to understand the reasons for oppression. I didn't want to commit suicide: indeed I didn't want to die at all, and I didn't want to be a witness to oppression. I wanted to live, grow, love, write, get pregnant, and be a mother. I wanted to taste happiness in the present, not in the past; I wanted happiness to be associated with the word "now," linked neither to heaven nor to a bygone past. That is how I finished writing my sister's story—with my grandmother's four words: Life is a right.

When my cousin Huda came to my house and made me the offer to go to Beirut, I accepted without thinking. Actually, I accepted after thinking for a long time, but all that thought had preceded Huda's visit to my house. It was as if her visit and her offer could see directly into my dreams. She wanted to distance me from the family and any talk about Henaa's long letter in which she talked about her relationship with Shawqi, the army officer who later became Huda's husband. She wanted to distance me from any disclosure that would destroy the marriage she'd waited for fifteen years to happen, after she'd already prepared her trousseau and locked it away in the cupboard. I also wanted to get far away. So I agreed to come here to live. I decided not to go back to Syria. I wanted to forget what happened. But I can't forget if I don't write about the past. I won't be the first woman who traveled abroad so she wouldn't die. My story can be added to the stories of women who leave their countries, travel abroad, or who are forced to leave. Oppression pushes women to emigrate, to flee: it's the kind of oppression that often comes in the form of a man. But my sister didn't see that she had any choice other than death, perhaps because with her boundless naiveté she believed that violence could sometimes be the other side of love.

I didn't hesitate to leave Syria for Lebanon. I left home with a suitcase filled with books, recordings of Asmahan's songs, and some clothes. I dreamed of writing freely without censorship. In Syria, my father used to receive Lebanese newspapers, some of which were later banned after the Assad family's coup, as part of what they called the Correction

Movement. I read all the books that my father had collected throughout his life. I started reading to him, first newspapers and then books too, after he got out of jail and had lost the desire to know what was happening around him in the outside world.

I had to tell the family what happened, but after Shawqi married my cousin Huda, it became difficult to talk. He was a young officer who aspired to social climbing that would help him reach a status closer to power. Marrying my sister—the daughter of an employee in a farming collective who'd just recently gotten out of prison—wouldn't secure this for him, whereas Huda was the daughter of a family who'd emigrated to the Gulf. Surely she was more appropriate for him, even if she was several years older than he was. He didn't even wait two weeks after Henaa's death to get engaged, and because it was still the mourning period he did so at a simple party with only family members present. I didn't go, I stayed home at my grandmother's; my legs and joints felt kind of paralyzed. I sat up in bed, rereading Henaa's letter. I don't know how many times I read it that evening. I needed to nourish the anger, which had started to grow inside me, and not let it atrophy and weaken me.

I felt at the time that my anger would keep me alive, but the silence almost consumed my heart and killed me. I remained silent for a year and then couldn't continue; I was no longer able to carry this anger around. My ability to absorb it had been exceeded. I let Huda know the truth during my visit to her after she'd given birth to her first child. I intended to visit her and tell her while she was breastfeeding her newborn.

As I was entering the building where she lived, I repeated the words that I would say to her in my head, imagining her response. She would be totally stunned, no doubt—perhaps she'd start crying and perhaps she'd ask for a divorce. But none of this happened. Huda acted as if she hadn't heard anything. As if what she'd heard was a story that happened to people she had no blood connection to, history with, or previous knowledge of. She kept listening, silently and calmly. This mystified me and made me think that Huda already knew.

I won't ever forget the day when Huda came to visit me. It was winter and cold outside. This was after I had gotten a job in the Ministry of Information and it emerged that the editorial department would be censoring and interfering with our work as journalists. Huda came alone. She asked my father's wife where I was and she indicated that I was in my room. She entered when I was writing, listening to Asmahan. When I saw her I lowered the sound of the music. She told me, "I know that you aren't happy with your job at the Ministry and you really want to be a journalist, writing without censorship. Why don't you go to Beirut, a place where you can write as freely as you like? You would be far away from this atmosphere. I'll help you as much as I can to keep your current job here, for a few months, while you're away. Take this money. Use it to set yourself up in your first year there, and I'll send you an amount that should be enough for you until you find work. This can all remain between the two of us. No one has to know about this or that I'm helping you. But I want you to destroy the letter, Henaa's letter."

I took the money from her without hesitating.

"I'll rip up the letter!" I found myself saying. "I'll do it the minute I leave Syria."

A quick idea flashed through my mind as I watched Huda get further and further away from the house, lost down the muddy, dark path—that my life after Henaa's death and my grandmother's death had become, despite the presence of my boyfriend, Suhayl, a dark tunnel; leaving the house and Syria was a lone ray of light. Suhayl couldn't understand my decision to leave Damascus or my need to move far away. He told me that I was making decisions without consulting him, as if he weren't there. All I wanted at that moment was to disappear and become invisible to everyone, including Suhayl.

But after everything that happened and these years, I still think about why Henaa didn't try to find another solution. Never in her life was Henaa a young woman who wasn't good at making decisions. What happens at that moment when a certain person decides to put an end to her life? My sister wasn't weak. I knew her completely. She was intelligent and had the ability to weigh things up much better than I did. In fact, she was always critical of my recklessness and emotionality. She described her relationship with Shawqi in detail in her letter. This description was written by a person who wouldn't commit suicide. She wrote: "At the end of the day, what is the meaning of love? What he told me is not what love is. I used to forget him too, when he was far away, as if he were a faint, passing dream. I used to desire him; sex with him was like being satiated after being really hungry. When I eat I forget what I ate, and I forget the hunger. And I knew deep down inside me that even if I call it love, this relationship has no future. I knew that I don't want the man I'm intimate with to be a father to my children. I knew that sooner or later I would be faced with such a situation. Now my pregnancy places me face to face with only one possible choice, or maybe two at the most."

What did Henaa mean by "only one possible choice, or maybe two at the most"? Was suicide one of these two choices? I didn't find an answer to this question. Did she try to find a solution and fail?

I used to watch my old Baathist father who'd been imprisoned and then repented sit in the house, fading each day. Shawqi would come into our house as the anointed king. It wasn't that difficult for him, especially as power had started to eat away at the mind and soul of my father's new wife. She used to be really pleased with the things that Shawqi brought home to us, and she was also the mother of the son my mother couldn't produce before her premature death. My half-brother, Atta, was my father's only pride and joy since it allowed him to finally be rid of the nickname he'd had for more than ten years—"Father of the two girls."

After Henaa committed suicide, no one in the family asked much about the real reasons for her death. They preferred silence. Silence is a social economy, but one providing neither supply nor investment, only losses that pile up and increase with time. They turned their eyes away from knowing anything. The price of the truth was too dear; no one wanted to pay it.

**

When I arrived in Beirut, the war hadn't yet started but the city was at the height of madness. After a few months, the madness increased and I started to feel as if I were in a social, political, and cultural cauldron: the Lebanese army's bombardment of fedayeen camps; the PLO Fatah movement's control over southern villages; general strikes; racy films; printing and selling books banned in other Arab countries; small tables at cafés witnessing global conflicts and wars between nations, noisy debates, and opposition parties; and the closing of roads, schools, and universities. Symposiums denouncing everything, the resignation of the government, the press on fire with clashing opinions: at this time, the war was preparing to change our destinies but we weren't aware of that yet.

It wasn't difficult at all for me to engage right away in this crowded hot mess that was called "media" in Beirut. Alongside working as a journalist, I enrolled in the English department at the university. I remember my first newspaper job, which seemed very odd and which I left less than a month after starting. Kemal Firat made fun of my naiveté when I told him about it. The newspaper was printed and stored in archives and not distributed in Beirut. I was told afterward that the owner of the newspaper printed them only for Iraqi embassies around the world. In my first interview with the paper's owner, he made clear that he needed a seasoned journalist, and I told him that I had only worked in journalism for a few months in Damascus. "That's all right," he said, and then he went abroad for a while, asking me to go in his office while he was gone and work on the archives, organizing the books and files on the shelves and in the small wooden cupboards. He gave me the keys to the cupboards and drawers and left. I went to the office and tried to organize what was there. I first organized the books on the shelves. I then started opening the locked drawers expecting to see back issues of the newspaper or minutes of meetings or articles that hadn't been published yet. But instead I found huge mounds of Playboy magazines, in addition to pornographic books and private photographs of the newspaper owner with different women in intimate settings.

Why had he asked me to organize his private archive when I had come looking for work as a journalist and not as a private secretary? Was this an invitation to enter into his personal life, and what would be the possible repercussions of this invitation? I wondered at the time. I decided to leave that job quickly without a fuss, to invent an excuse to get out of there. I returned everything to its place, and before locking the office I stole a black-and-white poster of the Russian pioneer astronaut Yuri Gagarin that I'd found in one of the cabinets rolled up and packed away in a cardboard tube. I felt no guilt about stealing it. Instead I felt confident that I was saving him. I saved Gagarin from the worst place he could have been put. Perhaps the best thing that I did in my first years in Beirut was to have stolen the Gagarin poster. That's because it didn't end at this point, but this little theft was the beginning of a journey of exploration and research about the life of the pioneer astronaut whose death in 1968 still resounded at the time. I kept collecting articles that dealt with his life and death. Kemal laughed and said that I had become specialized in this man with the smile that kept da Vinci and the Mona Lisa's special smile backstage.

Despite his smile, whenever I read an article about Gagarin I could feel his sadness wash over me. I wrote that it was not an accident that the student movement of 1968 had been born less than two months later. In some way it was a revolution against the murder of young people in the world, the murder of what he meant and stood for.

When I found a job at the BBC, I was like a child learning to walk. I had a lot to learn. I also had to write Henaa's story. I knew that I had to wait before I published it. I was afraid. I stayed afraid. They might do anything to silence me.

After I wrote about Henaa, I started to feel despair writing about dying young people, but I came to realize that good writing begins with despair. It's the compass of writing—that's when we know that the blue hour, that moment between twilight and darkness, dawn and morning light, is near and that words are waiting to come out into the light.

**

It rained all day long and I didn't leave the house. Echoes of the sounds of rain in Rummaneh appeared to me in a dream. So did memories of holidays in my grandmother Shahani's house, walking into her room, on cold early Eid mornings. I would crawl into her bed and sleep there. I don't know how many hours I spent there.

Rain here is different. It comes without the smell of the soil, exhaust pipes, and leftover fruits and vegetables left outside on wagons.

April 1977

My old friend Suhayl, whom I was in a relationship with during our university days in Damascus, snuck across the border from Syria into Lebanon weeks ago. He still hasn't found a way to retrieve his travel documents that the Syrian mukhabarat confiscated from him when he was arrested and detained for several months. His family was forced to pay to get him out of prison. He stayed a week at my place in Beirut, sleeping on the sofa in the spare room I used as an office. We spent much of this time in endless conversation. He told me that I had turned my back on him and come here to save myself alone without thinking of anyone else. I remember one day when he called to ask me if I wanted anything from the shops. I told him that I didn't need anything because I was planning to go out in the afternoon to have a drink on Hamra Street with a girlfriend of mine who wanted to take me out for my birthday and that I would be home for dinner.

Suhayl suggested that he join us.

He arrived after a bit, when the café was nearly full of customers. He was telling my friend about his plan to go to Sweden when one of the people sitting near us caught his attention. Dizzy with alcohol, this man was holding up his hand and saying in a loud voice to the man sitting across from him: "Two years ago, they made March 8 International Women's Day and Thatcher became the leader of her party. This was disastrous for us. Our wars started up then and haven't stopped."

"What's the connection?" the other man asked. "I don't understand!"

"Everything is connected to everything else," the first man replied, fidgeting in his seat as he was finishing what he was saying. "Isn't it enough that that bad luck year, 1975, began with Umm Kulthum dying. What a loss, her beautiful voice now buried in the ground."

Suhayl, who had stopped talking, was listening intently to these two men's conversation. Then he said, "Actually he's right ... but I really don't understand the Lebanese—when they're drunk they talk about the war and Thatcher too!"

When we asked for the bill at the end of the afternoon, the waiter walked over to us and said, while pointing at someone sitting behind us in the far corner, "It's taken care of. Him, over there." I turned and saw that it was Hani, one of the colleagues in my office who happened to have come into the café and, knowing it was my birthday, paid for our bottle of wine. Then he came over and chatted to me a bit, introducing himself to my girlfriend and to Suhayl, who turned his flush-red face away, stuffing his hands in his jeans pockets. I was so embarrassed that I quickly thanked Hani for coming over and then hurried to leave the café. I said goodbye to my friend, who walked back to her house nearby, and Suhayl and I walked away, looking for a car to take us home.

He didn't answer when I asked him why he didn't introduce himself and shake hands with Hani, though Hani had greeted him and held out his hand. He looked at me angrily. He told me that he thought we should have left the café from the moment the waiter told us that Hani had paid our bill. He added that I didn't respect him—what Hani had done diminished his manhood. Hani was tactless and lacking decency.

How could he have paid the bill when there was another man with me?

A soldier at a military checkpoint then motioned for the shared taxi taking us to my place to stop. The soldier was Syrian. He asked for the car's papers and the driver's ID card. Suhayl was nervous and looked at me, frightened. The anger faded from his eyes and I felt him coming closer to me, as if I were his mother, as if he would have hidden behind my skirt if he could. Whispering, I told him, "Stay calm." I took out my press card and told the security official that we were journalists. He didn't ask for Suhayl's ID card. We left. It was the beginning of the war, and the Syrian mukhabarat hadn't yet started to eliminate opposition journalists. I looked at Suhayl as he was breathing a sigh of relief, the flush in his face starting to fade.

At that moment, I found him repulsive. I hated his macho pretentions. "Where is your anger and your pride now? Did you leave them in the café, fighting against my peaceful colleague who just wanted to express his affection for me? For what?" I asked him sarcastically.

Suhayl nodded his head so I would stop talking and to express his resentment about what I'd said. In the taxi, I repeated the statement of the man from the café: "Everything is connected to everything else." I thought that this isn't just a passing comment here in Beirut. It isn't meaningless. It is reality—a reality of politics being connected to every day life, of ideas being connected to behavior, and of life being connected to death all the time.

That evening I prepared a simple dinner despite my anger—a salad, chicken, and mashed potatoes. Suhayl ate his food silently, and then sat and watched television while I took the empty plates into the kitchen and washed the dishes. I thought about the fact that this boring scene that I was now observing—the woman who prepares dinner and then washes the dishes while the man watches TV—was a far cry from my life. Despite being happy to see Suhayl and wanting to help him find a new life outside Syria, we had arrived at two different places in life that are impossible to reconcile. I briefly considered telling him about Kemal and our relationship. After what had happened at the café, however, I no longer felt that he could be a real friend to me.

While I was washing the dishes, Suhayl approached me, intending to rekindle our love affair, which was by now buried in time. He tried to kiss me, putting his hand on my breasts, as if those years that had passed far away from each other meant nothing to him, as if he believed that he had a retroactive right to my body and emotions. No doubt what had happened in the café, and then in the car, had affected his self-confidence and he now wanted to restore it through our sexual memories. I wondered at that moment how I'd ever loved him in the past. I pushed his hand away gently, averting my face.

"You are welcome in my house. You are a guest; I hope you act accordingly. But how do you believe that I could possibly desire you after what you did in the café? Your reaction to Hani's gesture was embarrassing and offended me. That's my business—he wanted to be nice to me on my birthday. It has nothing to do with you. Why do you want to involve yourself in something that has nothing to do with you? Because you're a man? And then there's your behavior at home." After a pause I added, angrily, "For a week you haven't even taken your own plate into the kitchen."

"Your obsession with women's rights and equality with men has eaten away at your brain. If you carry on like this you'll never find a man who desires to kiss you or put his hands on your breasts. Since you left Syria, you've distanced yourself from the core political causes that are more important than women's issues."

"You're talking rubbish, since I don't know any cause in the world that can be just and humane if it is not deeply connected to 'women's issues.' But it seems that what I'm saying has come too late, since all that still connects me to you are a few memories."

I was angry. I left Suhayl standing in the kitchen looking at me as if I'd come from outer space. I went into my room to try to regain some sense of calm.

**

I woke up in the morning and didn't find Suhayl. It seemed that he'd left early. There was an empty pot of Turkish coffee and a cup on the kitchen table. The blanket and pillow were still on the big sofa in the room where he'd been sleeping. I didn't find his suitcase there or his things in the bathroom.

April 1977

Last night Sabah stayed at my house. The bombing started and I couldn't let her leave, out of worry and fear. When the bombardment started up again at night, she jumped off the sofa bed in the office and came into my room. She stretched out next to me on the bed and couldn't fall back asleep. Then she was seized by laughter, when she started telling me the story of a woman who lived on the second floor of the building in Khandaq al-Ghamiq who used to refuse to remove her underwear when she was in bed with her husband for fear the bombardment would start and she wouldn't have enough time to get dressed before going down to the bomb shelter.

Sabah was used to the ground floor, where she felt safe. But my apartment was on a high floor, and staying there frightened her. Sometimes she seemed quite mad, and I wondered how she had all this energy throughout the day while plagued by constant anxiety. "Akh," Sabah said. Her "akh" rising up, elongated, distinctive, filled with a voice that wasn't yet hopeless, she continued, "If grief were a bank and paid interest, I'd be the richest person in the world!"

Since Sabah had started working in my home, she'd tell little bits about her life in Mardin each time she came. She arrived here young. But she hadn't forgotten anything. It's as if there are two lives inside of her—one here in Beirut, the other there in Mardin.

The only time I ever saw Sabah cheerful with that joy we so rarely find was at the dinner party after Kemal and I registered our marriage at the Turkish embassy. A few close friends had come to my place....

Sabah came and went, each time filling her cup with araq. Then, in the middle of the sitting room, she started dancing and spinning around and around like a whirling dervish. Soon she stopped in front of the poster of Yuri Gagarin hanging on the sitting room wall, contemplated it, and started speaking to him: "My heaven and hell are on this earth, I don't have any place but here. If they forced me to leave this earth, I would ask for a summer house in hell. All my dreams are there!"

When her auntie Fawziya arrived that evening and saw Sabah in the middle of the living room dancing, she started slapping her cheeks with the palms of her hands, saying, "The woman's gone mad! Good God, my brother's daughter has gone mad!" Sabah teetered over to her, hardly able to stand, grabbed the edges of Fawziyah's shirt, which totally covered her neck, and pulled them over each other. In a voice dripping with sarcasm, she said, "Cover up, sweetie, have you no shame…. There are men here. If I were you, I'd go home right now!"

While Fawziya stood there like a statue, stunned by what her niece was doing and saying, Sabah moved away from her and over to the picture of Gagarin, repeating, as her body tottered along with the rhythm of her voice, "Paradise is here…. This is heaven. I wish you were here."

Fawziya could no longer tolerate what Sabah was doing, so she suddenly got up to leave and scurried down the stairs, leaving the apartment door wide open behind her.

A few days later, Sabah's brother Moheiddine called her from Mardin, waking her up in the middle of the night to tell her that her auntie Fawziya had told her father that she had been dancing and drinking alcohol. After he'd finished speaking to his sister, her father had become terribly ill and took to his bed.

"He's sick?" Sabah started asking me angrily. "I wish he'd die. I wish fear and worry would consume him just as they ate away at my heart. He fell ill because I danced? He didn't fall ill when he married me off at fourteen, or when my husband, disappeared, or even when I didn't have a single cent, or when I had to divide all the money I had saved between the thieving 'good boys' who promised to bring back my husband and my father, who used my money to buy a house for my brother."

**

My boss liked my proposal to write about Mediterranean cities. This is how I met Kemal for the first time. I had to write about the legendary city of Istanbul, and Kemal showed it to me. In the evening, I suggested that we have dinner together on the Asian side. That is where he told me about a floating island, far away from Istanbul, that people don't visit and tourists don't yet go to. Throughout the course of the evening I learned that his stories about this island were a lure he was using to seduce me, and I was totally prepared to fall for this temptation despite my doubt that the island actually existed.

We parted at the end of the evening after his friend Taymour picked us up in his car to drop me back at my hotel on Istiklal Street. As he pulled over so I could get out, I heard Kemal answering his friend, who'd just spontaneously proposed that we all go and have another drink somewhere, "No, we aren't going to have another drink, we have to go, our women are waiting for us!" I told myself that he was tactless and ill-mannered. But surely I also felt jealous, jealous of the woman whom a man rushes to be with at night. And not just any man, but this specific man! I walked away from the car extremely slowly, rummaging in the bottom of my handbag nervously for my hotel room key, not finding it easily.

Before my second visit to Istanbul, we had exchanged a number of letters and were cultivating a close, solid friendship. On the way to the Turkish airport, I sat next to him in his little Fiat; he turned on the motor, saying nothing. The car started and I said nothing either. Through our silence, we were reminiscing about all the words we'd exchanged in long letters. This reminiscing was like returning to the passion lying dormant within us. There was something ablaze in that cramped space. The air coming through the partially closed window added tame pulsations to the silence between us. "It's going to be a long day," Kemal said, breaking the silence. "Istanbul needs weeks, one week is not enough. You should move here and stay with me."

**

There is another memory of Istanbul that I didn't experience and that doesn't require personal experience. This is a memory from history books that don't put Istanbul in the friend category, a memory associated with the language of Ottoman or Turkish soldiers that doesn't care that Nazim Hekmat and Yashar Kemal also wrote in this language. This memory became a topic of discussion between us, Kemal and me. In those days that we passed together in Istanbul, I saw the city with new eyes. But it isn't easy to hold history accountable and also recover another history that has yet to be written: with time, such a recovery becomes the heart of a new reading of a relationship, a memory, a city. Did the people who write history walk in the streets of Istanbul first? This personal relationship with any given city is like entering history through countless, endless gates. This is how I started walking around, searching for present-day connections with the past. My geographical worlds all arrive at Istanbul. I wanted to reorganize my memory, and my collective memory as well.

There are hidden similarities between Damascus, Beirut, and Istanbul. They have a shared history of travellers, stories, culture, and mood; they are cities of pluralism and successive civilizations. Can any history of Beirut or Damascus be written without first returning to Istanbul? I walk around, searching for signs that link Mediterranean cities together, for comparable lifestyles or comparable violence. Do people in this city live through violence like they do in our countries?

I searched for answers to my questions by watching people in the city where violence starts in the street. They must also live with anxiety, like the anxiety in Beirut or that born of repression in Damascus. I reflected on this as we went to discover the walls of ancient Constantinople, followed by a stroll along the banks of the Bosphorus, with Kemal talking to me about the apocalyptic notion ingrained in people's minds in Istanbul that a big earthquake—at least 8.0 on the Richter Scale—will hit one day, and the number of victims will be in the hundreds of thousands. Earthquake experts agree that there are two fault lines in Istanbul. This is a legend of fear and uncertainty, I said, as he pointed toward the sea, the surface of which was sparkling with the lights of the city from its gentle hills. The Sea of Marmara lies in front of the walls of Constantinople; on the other side are the Princes' Islands. People are expecting this big earthquake to happen within fifty years.

As I listened to Kemal, I thought about Damascus, where I was born; and Beirut, my second home. People in Beirut live in the heart of the apocalypse, whereas in Istanbul they are expecting it. In Damascus, they delude themselves with false reassurances. In Beirut, people are trying to escape the apocalyptic, in Istanbul they are fearfully waiting to enter into it. In Beirut, as in Istanbul, everyone is at a way station, Damascus is somewhere between the two. Fear is everywhere, no?

Sometimes when I observed the color of Kemal's eyes, I would notice how it changed with the earth's movement around the sun. He would smile and gently approach me, touching my arm lightly and saying in a calm, warm voice, "Noura ... All of your questions are anxious. I understand that but let's leave time to time."

Then he asked me, "Can't you extend your stay for another week?"

"I don't know, I'll see," I responded, thinking about what he'd said and telling myself that I might have found something with this man whom I met a few months earlier. Tenderness filled me when I stood near him—tenderness toward him and toward the sky, which everyone shares despite their violence, and the sea that swallowed the earth's secrets. My heart is warm. I heard my inner voice as we exchanged a fleeting kiss for seconds, which felt as though they summed up an entire lifetime. All of a sudden I remembered Shahani, my grandmother, and almost laughed. I told him that his words, "Let's leave time to time," made me remember her: they were somehow alike despite their differences. Kemal seemed to me both nomadic and cosmopolitan: characteristics that his adaptable personality made coexist within one person. I told him about Shahani's origins, her childhood, and her voyage to the mountains, where she became a primary school teacher and married my grandfather. I felt strongly that if he had been able to meet her, he would have found in her a lot of what he'd lost. Perhaps he would have found her wisdom that had matured without losing any of the vibrant, original feelings that made life a constant surprise. But also he would have found great richness in their shared culture. They would have been friends. I travelled to this city with which I had an ambivalent, tenuous, and complex relationship. It's a relationship linked to a fading memory passed down by Shahani, my grandmother of Armenian origin. But the moment I arrived and walked in the streets, I discovered that this journey of mine was a rereading of history—my grandmother's history, people's history, our history.

I would never have arrived at this had Kemal not been with me. With him, my doubts about history books started to gain power and take on new meaning.

**

It is a very hot spring. Four days without water or electricity. A pungent heat and violent bombardment impact the neighborhood. Beirut, which in one of my articles I once called "the city that doesn't sleep," has now become "the neighbor of death."

Sabah wouldn't leave her house. She said the fighters would occupy it the moment she left. She spent her time between her house and that of Ibrahim, who lost his wife. It's not enough that a woman here should be the wife of someone who was disappeared, but she had to expose herself to death every day simply to maintain her home. She kept looking after her little garden in Khandaq al-Ghamiq despite the bombs falling all around it.

"Where would I go?" Sabah asked me. "I want to stay and die here."

She feared that if she left the building like those other residents who had and had no one left there, her kidnapped husband wouldn't be able find her when he returned. I looked over and saw her standing in front of the bookshelves in the sitting room of my flat, taking a book, opening it, and slowly pronouncing the words. At that moment, I felt that she knew deep down that he wouldn't return. It is difficult for her to deal with this—as if it's a fact, the truth. Because if she does admit it to herself, she will feel so much sadder and more defeated. Accepting that her husband won't ever return would be like his second death. She wanted to accept her loneliness without pain. She didn't want to go back to Mardin or to search for another safer place in Beirut. She is attached to this place, which is witness to two worlds, two regions, two memories, and two times. She wanted to remain the watch-woman of a place on the edge. The edge of nowhere.

Sabah fascinates me. It is not fascination in the recognized, creative sense of the word, associated with people who present themselves as out of the ordinary. She fascinates me as she is: a human mixture of wisdom, madness, innocence, sixth sense, love of life and sorrow. Everything about her seems like parts of a timeless mosaic. As she is, she gives me strength and desire … to be near her.

**

Kamal Jumblatt was assassinated a few months ago. It wasn't an ordinary murder. It was a murder intended to kill Lebanon as a whole. What is frightening is the silence. A terrifying silence. Here in Beirut, and also in Damascus.

Last fall, someone tried to assassinate Raymond Eddé. The attempt failed. Everyone knew who did it. Eddé left his city, a city he loved, and emigrated.

**

We are in Beirut, which means we live at the edge of death every day. We stand between the city's mutilated life and its inevitable death: we keep having to choose between death and life with no pulse. We must choose between living on with its face mutilated, or without a face at all.

**

In her long letter, Henaa asked how it was that no one ever noticed the relationship between her and Shawqi, which they'd been carrying on in our house in Damascus. He played backgammon with our dad, who really liked him and would look out from time to time for the car in front of our old building, where a driver would wait for our guest for hours. He started eating and drinking with us, and my father's wife didn't think it strange if he was in the house even if my father wasn't home. Slowly he became like one of the family, and no one noticed the transformation that occurred when we started treating him like one of us. He helped my father wipe his record clean after he got out of prison, and then found him a job as an administrator in the central post office. When I was at the university, my brother at school, my father's wife out visiting, and my father at work, he would come in and go straight to Henaa's room, where she'd be waiting for him. He would take her quickly. When he entered her, he would put the side of his hand between her teeth and she would bite down when she had an orgasm. She wasn't afraid with him, she wrote. She used to wait for him.

She added that her intellect couldn't accept their relationship; she couldn't stand listening to him talking politics with our father. But this didn't prevent her from doing what she was doing with him. She called it a fling, one that would end someday, but she didn't take into account the possible result—that a pregnancy would change everything. Suddenly there was the imminent risk of the relationship changing from being a secret to being open, from a light, passing whim to the heavy permanence of reality.

Henaa, preferring to spare her family the curse of killing her, chose to do the job herself. She wrote naively that not everyone is brave enough to commit suicide.

But suicide doesn't require bravery as much as hope, I thought while rereading the letter.

**

Hope requires bravery, that's true, but living in Beirut takes even more bravery.

Facing up to other people and questioning them is easy. What's hard is when you must question and face up to yourself! When there are no masks, when there's nothing but your eyes and your naked skin.

This city exposes the individual. It allows you, accidentally perhaps, to be an individual—though you always are there within a larger sea, in which you only exist by belonging to a sect masquerading as a political party or an extended family. Various, disparate, contradictory, with diverse cultures and social backgrounds, Beirut—which at times is distant from itself—can be everything to everyone. But at the same time, it isn't like anything but itself. In Beirut you have to face only yourself alone.

This city is the heart of life, and it keeps dancing on its wounds. Despite this, I didn't feel as free in the past as I feel now. A freedom of movement and walking makes me feel a levity I never felt previously. In Beirut, there is a place for everyone. There is a place to dance on my own wounds, too.

**

Feelings of loneliness. No letters from Kemal. Most of my colleagues at work have gone abroad on holiday, and I am alone
in Beirut, with its endless explosions.

**

My feelings of loneliness take on another flavor when I walk
in the Beirut rain. I let it dampen my hair, handbag, and
clothes…. I start running, not fleeing the bombardment but
rejoicing in the raindrops, and listening to my voice singing
like a bird. No doubt I'm in love.

**

Instead of finishing my article, I started looking at Kemal
sitting at the table writing his political op-ed by hand, one
word flowing out after the other. I realized that this was his
way of being sure that his sentences wouldn't escape him
and his conflicting thoughts would find a way out and be
able to breathe. They would stay there and not fall between
the cracks amid his exhausted panting. I laughed, trying to
decipher the letters of his words mixed between French and
Turkish. "Talismans," I said, understanding some of them,
but after a while I surrendered to sleepiness. He was writing
about Turkey, how it didn't learn anything from the war. He
wrote, "We lost along with Germany and then we reverted to
nationalism, idolatry, and militarism."

I think that we—Kemal and I—are both stuck between the West, which decided our fates, and the devastating past. We don't know how to find a way out. Being from two neighboring countries, we share an enormous amount of loss but are different in how we deal with our losses. He still needs compensation for them, whereas every day that carries less of a loss than the day before is a celebration for me. But we came together despite this difference. I find it difficult to define precisely what bonds us together, perhaps our consciousness of that loss.

He writes to me and I write about him. Each of us needs the other; we are each committed to our own story. After our first sexual encounter, I told him, "I am not in love with you, but our relationship is comfortable and doesn't make my head hurt." He laughed and said, "Look at you, all defensive, brandishing your weapons before even arriving at the battle. You're a coward—you won't ever be able to love. Love requires you to put down your weapons, to accept loss. Accepting loss is part of love itself."

At that time, I was still afraid of love—it caused death. It caused my sister's death.

**

On the last day of Kemal's visit to Beirut, a few hours before he left, the waiter in the restaurant was standing next to us. Before he brought the food, Kemal asked me to close my eyes. Only at the cinema, I felt, had I ever experienced what was happening to me at this moment. Never had I thought that

151

one day it could happen to me. Kemal touched my hand and pulled it toward him; my fingers felt a piece of metal. I opened my eyes and found that he had taken a ring out of a small box, a ring that was a green-eyed snake wrapped around itself. Laughingly, he said, "I made a ring for you out of the snake from the Garden of Eden!"

**

When Kemal comes back to Beirut, I will give him this note-book that is now almost full. I am writing about my daily life whenever I find the time. I told Sabah that I must write so I don't forget anything when he comes.

This is a challenge for me, to write completely freely about him and me and the two of us together, but at the same time knowing that he will read everything I wrote when he returns. I write as freely as I can, knowing that what I am writing will soon be before his eyes.

**

The article I wrote about the second anniversary of the Lebanese war did not please my boss. In my meeting with him today he said he'd wanted me to mention the numbers of victims and those displaced. But what kind of memory is that? I wrote lovingly about my memory of the city that embraced me, in which I was reborn in what I dare call my true birth. This is a memory not only of violence but also of love—a memory of friends I worked with who left, a memory of people, like me, who still dream of change. It is a memory of people who hid their neighbors out of fear of sectarian violence against them. I told him that the war came, yes, but it will end soon never to return. He considered me an inexperienced journalist when I said these words. He advised me to write a novel or short stories. These kinds of comments made me angry. But his words did make me think about those people who don't write, draw, or practice any form of art. What do they do? How do they express, today, the memory of violence that they witnessed and lived then?

Before the director had even finished talking to me at our meeting, I mused that excess idealism is a good excuse to avoid fighting for life and to avoid living life profoundly. It's also why we don't see what is happening around us. He won't let me go with the photographer to the South tomorrow!

I feel the continual turmoil of what's happening in Lebanon. I am no longer sure of anything in the face of the real, actual, daily violence that's incomparable to anything you can imagine.

[...]

**

I felt tense for days after my family's phone calls, when they'd learned that I'd published Henaa's story. I didn't want to go to work. I asked Sabah to go to the office a number of times to bring me the international papers or when I really needed to send an article quickly. "The only thing I have done for you up until now is replace you in the office," she commented, laughing. "Tomorrow they'll forget me," I responded. "Shawqi won't chase me my whole life. He'll grow up, have other concerns, and forget me."

But I soon came to realize that Shawqi's loathing toward me only increased with the number of stars he accumulated on his shoulders. It's a strange dynamic, the relationship between obedience and humiliation, cruelty and power.

But what does he want from me? Why did he come to Lebanon? Why him specifically? All of a sudden one day I saw him in front of a university building when I was walking out of the main gate with my colleagues. He smiled and asked me, "Where are you going to go to escape from me?" Mockingly, he told me he loved poetry and was visiting a poet who lived nearby. A mukhabarat officer with a taste for poetry, and a poet who befriends a mukhabarat officer? *The surreal misery that's become reality*, I thought while running down the stairs to get to the street. From that day on, I started fearing him. Before that I wasn't afraid. Perhaps it's because I hadn't ever before seen such an enormous number of soldiers and military checkpoints in Beirut, and at its main entry points.

Kemal told me on the phone that night, "They've entered Lebanon and aren't going to leave for a long time."

... 1978
[...]
Then Kemal wrote me that we'd have two houses in Turkey: a little house near the sea in Izmir and another one in Istanbul. Kemal didn't mention my house here in Beirut. I don't want to leave Beirut. It's my home; I feel that I'm invisible here. "I

154

know that I have many homes but I feel that my true home is where I never am," I answered him.

**

There is no historical moment in our miserable history, I think. There is nothing. What is called "historical" in history books changes with every coup d'état and is just bubbles of lies—self-loathing, harm, and destruction. These bubbles of lies breed and grow, and words grow alongside them that take our sight away so that we can no longer see devastation. With the seizure of power in Syria, pictures of the old despotism were exchanged for pictures of the new one. The present changed into a sole ruler. People don't think about the contempt with which they are treated every day. This history repeats itself in every Arab country.

**

Sabah worries me when she's extremely depressed. She grows silent and stops eating during the day. When she's hungry she eats fresh thyme leaves. Yesterday she just put cardamom pods in her mouth and didn't eat anything at all. Today she suddenly stopped reading the sentences I'd written for her and asked me if I loved Kemal. Her question surprised me. I realized that despite all this time having passed, I was still a prisoner of my family tragedy in Syria: my sister's suicide, my escape … yes, I still call it an escape though officially it is referred to differently—"travelling to work where there is a freer press," or "studying English literature." But, at the end of the day, it was an escape. I was unable to cope with enormous evil. This evil aroused the feelings of my family, which swam about in it happily. It's as if my sister's death had been meaningless, or simply the preparation for another death, like sharpening the blade of a knife for another round of evil. It was important to publish the story of her suicide, many years after I'd written it and filed it among my other papers. I included a number of passages from Henaa's letter in the story. Kemal encouraged me to publish it. He crushed my fear when he told me, "Look at yourself! Your silence is a poison slowly killing you.... Speak up!"

But why am I thinking about all of this now when Sabah's question was if I loved Kemal?...

I told her that love is being always ready to leave. She asked me again, enunciating her words slowly and seriously, as if asking me to stop "philosophizing" for a bit, as she would put it, and to just answer simply and directly. I thought about the times Kemal and I spent together during his many visits to Beirut. He would come, leave, and then come back.

This swinging back and forth between longing and being together, between waiting and connecting—a connection always followed by emptiness akin to a little death. "Yes, I love him.... But at the same time I am completely prepared to split up."

Sabah looked at me in the wandering way I'd grown used to. She seemed to be trying to regain words to frame them within some experience she'd lived herself. Then she uttered the sentence that she never stopped using: "Ah, life is leaving and loss."

She took a long drag on her cigarette as if it were her only source of air.

**

Yesterday I asked Kemal if there were mosques in Turkey named after Ataturk. He scoffed at my question, drowning in laughter, and saying, "Of course not!" He added that this question hadn't even occurred to anyone in Turkey, ever. He called Taymour to tell him I'd asked this and Taymour promised he'd write an article about it!

**

It's been raining for days in Beirut, sometimes with a little ray of sunshine, shining through for moments and disappearing. The weather is cold and cloudy; people haven't seen it like this for a long time. It surprises them, especially in villages not too far above sea level that usually have moderate temperatures. The children are happy because it snowed. They'd never seen snow before. I dreamed of visiting Rummaneh, my mother's village in Syria, where my grandmother lived. But how can I, after everything that's happened?

February 1978

I regret my moments of bad temper during our conversations when we were together. My anger is tied to memories that have nothing to do with Kemal, nothing to do with our love.

Those memories are only negative things that have piled up, one after another, and weighed heavily on my heart, making me misunderstand what he wanted to say. They're all things related to male dominance. I know that sometimes he interferes in my life and work for no reason other than the intensity of his love for me. But this worries me. Close intimacy worries me and makes me feel uncomfortable. I need a lot of time to understand that our intimate relationship might be different from my relationship with Suhayl, that it's far removed from a man's desire for control and ownership.

I will tell him when we meet that my anxiety that he sometimes saw when he was here is because I am completely exposed to him. Not only did I expose my body, but also my worries and fears. I will ask him to accept this way of being exposed as it is, to be patient. And in turn I will try to accept both his irrational fear of losing me, and also his jealousy, which I sometimes can't bear. [...]

**

A regular Sunday afternoon. A calm Beirut. Despite this, I feel death approaching. We spend time cheating death. Then, after a while, we start adding up our losses.

I go to the kitchen to prepare a delicious soup for dinner, nonetheless.

I couldn't find tahini to make mutabbal. I didn't find any at Sabah's place either. So I told myself encouragingly, *Why don't I use sesame? It's the primary ingredient, after all. Isn't tahini extracted from sesame?*

I ground up five tablespoons' worth in the coffee grinder stored up on a high shelf that I hadn't used in a long time, and then added some water. It was delicious.

March 1978

Today Taymour visited me, with a gift and a letter from Kemal. He told me about their trip to Ankara, about their comrades, and about other people there, but Taymour can't tell stories like Kemal can. He is objective and focuses more on what he's seen with his own eyes, whereas Kemal rewrites the whole world when he tells me his stories. He concentrates on those tiny things that life is made of. Taymour left after I gave him my letter. In it, I wrote that I want Kemal to tell me everything when we meet, since I'm not satisfied by Taymour's stories at all.

I wrote the letter while lying in bed. I was looking at my belly and I was feeling it grow rounder today. I was naked when I wrote to him. I don't want to cover up any of myself in front of him. It is bad enough that he is far away and that words are all that connects me to him. It's bad enough that we have them between us. I love my body when I write to him naked. I think about how it's connected to him; in a way it's connected to him alone. Strange how I don't think about anyone anymore since my belly started growing. It's as if our child growing inside me takes not only my nourishment but also my sexual fantasies and swallows them. It devours my thoughts, blood, and other bodily fluids.

My child is Kemal in some way.

I made my room into a beautiful place for my son and me to live in after he is born. I am remembering my grandmother Shahani, often now. Everything that happened in her lifetime implied misery—in 1940, she lost my grandfather who'd traveled to Palestine to fight the British and died there, finding herself all alone and responsible for two children: my mother and my uncle. It was a hard life, but she succeeded in creating a parallel world that no one could take away from her. She was indefatigable even as she was dying. She told me, "Noura, the places that you live mirror you, so wherever you go, make the place your own and hang onto the radiance of your soul."

**

Every word I write, I want Kemal to read when he visits Beirut. In writing, I attempt to go deeper, to be freer. It's a challenge to write freely about what's in my head without fearing that what I write will be misunderstood. Indeed even if I'm misunderstood there's always a chance for discussion. This is much of what attracted me to Kemal—that open space for conversation with no attempt to twist words around to make them dull and neutral.

The idea that he will read everything I write turns me on. It's a bit like sharing nakedness—sharing a special naked desire with him. I seduce him when he's far away; I seduce him with what I write to him. It's something exciting strengthening the pulse of my desire. His eyes will see what I write, even if, while I'm writing, I'm in one of those states of desperation that have afflicted me since my sister's death.

He knows that we wish to remain far from the eyes of others when we write of our despair. But here I am naked in front of him, naked with only pen and paper. I want to be a crystal that reflects unique lights in its transparency, absorbing the outside world and reflecting back only its own shape. Kemal will definitely see my reflection when he reads. He'll feel the halo of its embrace, and also how its power is reflected.

**

I am writing everything here and he will read it: I'm afraid to move to Turkey with him; the difference in language frightens me. The idea of being in a place where I don't understand the language makes me feel anxious. For me, a third language is like a station stop that I can't always see as a reality. And then there are the things that are difficult to reach because of what this third language erases between us. Sometimes mountains of misunderstandings pile up because of a language whose words we have to think a lot about before speaking. He knows how I feel. He also knows that having conversations with people in English isn't enough for me. He knows that it's not enough simply to learn how to hail a taxi or go shopping. I want to listen to the news, read newspapers and books—literary and political works—in his language. I want to understand fluently what is written. I want us not simply to remain in two different worlds, meeting through a language that's not ours. And what language will we speak with our child, who will be born soon?

April 1978

I need an entire life, perhaps another life, in order to under-stand why there's all this violence. Today at work one of the women journalists newly arrived from London said that the civil war in Lebanon is a negative expression of the intimate relationship between the Lebanese sects, which are impossible to get rid of. My colleague Hani interfered laughingly, "That means hatred is the highest form of admiration, so the highest form of admiration is shelling and bombing each other, no?"

Their conversation, which from a distance seemed superficial and illogical, made me think about the crimes that Lebanese people have perpetrated against each other, especially those in which the murderer and his victim had what were considered to be good neighbourly relations. I don't know how at a given moment, the people who had these good relationships exchanged gifts of hatred, with an unlimited murderous passion.

May 1978

I am looking at the pictures that we took together at the sea-side, pictures in which we're smiling. They're beautiful, full of love and a largely serene mood. Yesterday evening, after Kemal left Beirut for Istanbul, time passed that I didn't know what to do with. I could neither sleep nor wake up. Feelings of emptiness pervaded my consciousness, and it took a great effort to regain my sense of self. His call came at a time when I needed to hear his voice. The phones in Beirut were working normally without cutting off. This has been rare since the beginning of the war. Hearing his voice was like a caress, as if I could smell his scent.

I slept a little bit in the afternoon so I'd be able to stay up late in the office at night. I've asked to change my work hours in a few months, after my child is born. I haven't had a response yet. I woke up at the beginning of the evening and read Kemal's last letter. It arrived hours after he left. He wrote it and sent it to me before he arrived in Beirut. As if I could retrieve him by reading a letter written before his arrival.

After he left, Sabah commented that the two of us, Kemal and I, were made to be together. She liked him not because he was from her country, but because he awakened in her soul both the kindness of friends and the warmth of family that she'd lost when she came to Beirut.

June 1978

Sabah and I agreed that she would come every day after my baby was born. She is the only one I trust here. She knows how to take care of babies very well, even though she doesn't have children of her own. In Mardin, she used to help her mother look after her brother Moheiddine when he was a baby. She used to prepare his food and bathe him, despite their miniscule age difference. Girls grow up quickly—they become women early on and take on household and childrearing responsibilities. Sabah used to come over every evening since I started teaching her to read and write. She'd sit near me on the sofa while I wrote. I'd leave her to write down words in her notebook, trying to read and compose sentences. Of course the first sentence she wanted to learn to write was, "Life is leaving and loss." When she saw her famous sentence in front of her she laughed from a place so deep within her soul that she cried. She was like someone who'd found her missing beloved in her arms.

**

Sabah came to Beirut young. The war started not long after. Perhaps only a few years later—she's not good at specifying dates. The city remained beautiful despite it. But it's not like Istanbul, Sabah would say. Beirut is like one of Istanbul's neighborhoods. She'd visited Istanbul once for only four days, with her boyfriend Ahmed, who left her and emigrated to Germany. She kept longing for him and would cry in my flat. I told her to let it go and relax a bit. I made us two cups of tea and invited her to sit down. "The best way to forget a man who left you is to convince yourself that he's dead," I told her. As she wiped away her tears, she said, reluctantly, "The first Ahmed died, he died…. But what about the second? Will he ever come back?" She asked this looking at me, as I moved my hands around, raising them up in front of me, joking in our own way—I would act as though I were getting ready to fight her. Her crying transformed into muttering, and then a laugh she didn't expect or know the source of, even while she had tears still shining in her eyes like drops of light. We burst out in unstoppable laughter together, and I told her, "Forget everything.... Forget it, Sabah. Otherwise how will a third Ahmed find his way to you?!"

"We're cousins," Sabah told me, as if she wanted to secure a blood relation between us. "Your grandmother Shahani is from Mardin, the region I come from."

Actually, we are migrant women, I tell myself, migrants as invisible as the places we live in. We don't see these cities, but rather we see something of our own cities in every corner that reminds us of them.

The year that Sabah came to Beirut, she lived with her husband's family and her auntie but she soon couldn't bear living with them. So she and her husband moved to the building in Khandaq al-Ghamiq, where he found work as its caretaker.

When we met, she seemed lonely. In spite of everything, however, she stayed strong. Her friend Mariam would visit her from time to time, and whenever she would cry, Mariam would start repeating loudly, "You're not going to be weak, Sabah. You're going to stay strong." Once, when I was in her house eating a meal she'd prepared especially for the two of us, her auntie Fawziya came over asking her to come back and live with her because the two of them were both alone now. She told her that it isn't becoming for a woman to live alone, and that her brother, Sabah's father, won't stop calling her to try to get his daughter to move in with her aunt. Sabah lost her patience that day, and opened the door to her auntie so she'd go back home, wishing her a long life as she left. "What's it to her if I live alone?" Sabah asked me. "And since when does my father care about me? He doesn't ask about me unless he needs money!"

Then she started cursing the minute she'd opened the door to her auntie in the first place.

**

Whenever Sabah came over to my apartment, she'd stand in front of the poster of Gagarin, looking at him and flirting with him. When I told her his story, she cried. She told me she didn't like hearing stories about people dying young. Dying young means there's no way you can deal with anything. It's exactly like someone we love who has been disappeared. "Isn't being disappeared, in some way, dying young?" She asked me.

I hung the poster of Gagarin on the wall of the living room after I stole it from the office of the newspaper owner who printed his papers but never distributed them. The color of the paint on the wall around the poster had faded and yellowed, some of it having flaked off around the edges. The humidity all along my apartment's walls left swirling gray-brown stains on the poster. The upper part of the picture was damaged. Humidity had eaten away at the edges near Gagarin's eyes and forehead. Despite all this, his smile still hinted at the freshness of that timeless moment.

I took it off the wall and carried it to Sabah's house one evening. I told her, jokingly, "This handsome man wants to be near you, and his smile keeps following you. Hang it up on your wall."

Sabah was happy with Gagarin and asked where to hang him. She didn't want to put him in the bedroom near the picture of her disappeared husband. She thought she wouldn't be able to stand there and smile at the poster while her husband's eyes stared out at her. She decided to try to find Gagarin a place far away. Finally, she located a wall in the short corridor connecting the sitting room to the kitchen. That way she'd see Gagarin every time she passed by, coming and going. She could then return his every smile with two of hers.

Sabah told the women in the building that this man was a relative of hers killed in the war. "Finally, Gagarin's smile is hanging on the walls of Khandaq al-Ghamiq," I told her afterward, but Sabah looked at me and seemed surprised by what I'd said. Perhaps she herself believed that the man in the picture was a relative of hers and not Gagarin. Perhaps a day would come when Sabah would tell me the story of her relative in the picture and how he died in a burning airplane!

**

In his last letters, Kemal seemed to have lost any life for hope. In one, he wrote, "It is the tenth anniversary of May 1968, and nothing remains of it now except 69.... I'm referring to the sexual meaning of the number."

No doubt he had drunk a lot of raki before writing this. No doubt he was laughing bleakly, too, that dark laugh of his I'd gotten used to, filled with painful sarcasm, which reveals flaming gray feelings, devoid of any joy.

**

I'm waiting for Kemal and I don't know when we'll meet again. In his last letter he said he would be here in July. I haven't chosen a baby name yet; I will do so when Kemal gets here. I wanted a girl, and when the doctor informed me that I was carrying a boy, I started trying to think of boys' names. I knew that if it had been a girl, her name would have been Shahani. Shahani is the name that my grandmother couldn't use in her life. Right now I'm thinking about the name Karim, but I want Kemal to participate in that decision with me.

**

My brother Atta called me today on the public phone and said to me, "Don't come to Damascus! They want your head. First and foremost, Shawqi, whom I've started to wish were dead. He is the instigator. He fabricated stories about you, and I wouldn't rule out the possibility that he's also sent reports back home about your doings in Beirut. They arrested your comrades. Hazem, Nada, and Haitham have been sent to prison. Don't ever come! Shawqi heard about the story you published. We are afraid of his reaction when he gets the magazine. You've destroyed our family. I wish you …" I didn't want to hear any more, so I interrupted him: "Why do they want my head? Isn't my sister's head enough for them?" I asked him that … and then I cried.

11
SEPTEMBER 1994

Maya sat next to Sarah, who was driving the car slowly. No words broke the morning silence. Going out on Sunday mornings was what Maya loved most, because the roads were free of cars. She started looking silently out the window, horrified at how the sea road had changed—the land around it had lost most of its trees. The slopes near the sea had transformed from green forests to a cement jungle.

Since her return to Beirut, Maya hadn't had the chance to see Sarah as much as she should have or to spend weekends with her and Shadi, who wanted to go to the seaside. She also really felt the need to break off from her family and her weekly visit to Nada's house for lunch. Since returning to Lebanon, and Zeyad being hospitalized and then passing away, she hadn't spent one day free, like today. Her return in these circumstances had left her feeling a loss much greater than the one she'd felt in Paris.

On the coastal road, they had to pass through a number of military checkpoints before arriving at the sandy beach in Sour. Maya turned around to the backseat, where Shadi was sitting; she wanted to hug him and caress him when she saw that he'd fallen back asleep like an angel. She woke him up early that morning. She held his hand and it warmed her heart. His little hand made her feel safe in a way that now she still missed from time to time. She turned back around to face forward and closed her eyes herself. Maya recalled moments of waking up early and the sight of the morning clouds banished by the first rays of the sun that pushed them back, far out of sight. A timid happiness flooded her entire being.

"This is my place here," Maya said, pointing out the car window at the beach. Surprised, Shadi asked her if she was born here. She shook her head no, explaining that we can be enamored of places to which we have no previous family connection. We can be enamored of a place and it can become ours. We can develop a lifelong attachment to it that needs no justification. Sarah parked the car near the entrance to the beach. Little tents were scattered on the sand. Fairouz's morning songs echoed through the place. It was the end of summer and people had started not coming to the beach. Sarah chose a tent that she found a bit farther away from the few tents already standing, and then asked the young man working there to move a table and chairs to a spot as near to the sea as possible. "It seems we've gotten here early, it's not yet past ten," Maya said, sounding slightly happy. It is easy to see the horizon when there aren't any other beachgoers.

On the few occasions when Sarah visited Paris to meet Maya, it was as if their friendship hadn't been affected by time and distance at all. Once they got together they'd start talking and acting as though they'd seen each other the day before. There was a lot to say. They always jumped in straightaway to spontaneously exposing and expressing their hidden, inner selves. One word followed another, and there, at the sea, it took only the first beer to complete the conversation.

Sitting there now beside the sea, Maya told Sarah about what she'd found in Noura's diaries, about meeting Sabah, and about the murder of Noura and her son in an explosion in 1978. She also told her about Kemal's letters, which had made her feel connected to this man in some way, but she didn't know how. "There's something connecting me to Noura too," Maya continued. "Her death didn't allow her to finish writing what she wanted to. I've only found notebooks full of her diaries. And isn't it odd that I found diaries of a woman with whom I'm connected by such a strong bond—is it the love of Asmahan's voice? She came from Damascus with a suitcase filled with recordings of Asmahan's songs. But why haven't I yet seen a picture of her among the dozens of photos I've found? With every page of her diary, I try to imagine her face and her shape, and with every love letter from Kemal I try to picture her body, her hair, her eyes. But I've failed."

Sarah listened attentively and then asked, as if to bring Maya back to reality, "After the film, then what? How will you live? Nada is right. Think a bit about the situation; we have to find you a stable job."

"I have enough material for the book on Asmahan. The lost stories and lives of people fascinate me—the ones who died mysteriously."

Maya thought about Noura's diaries, everything this woman had collected and written about the pioneer astronaut Yuri Gagarin.

"I can't stop thinking that if Yuri Gagarin and Asmahan were still alive today, perhaps they'd have met and become the most important lovers in history despite their age difference. I wish this meeting had happened."

Laughing, Sarah said, "You haven't changed…. Living abroad hasn't changed you at all! Your imagination is still vivid, thank God! Writing about the hidden, mysterious lives of people is your dream, I know that, but I am talking about work and income, Shadi's life, his schooling, and his needs!"

"I know very well what I am doing is not considered work from a financial point of view, but this is my passion. I will find work, of course, alongside this. I care about the lives of people wherever they come from and whatever social class they belong to. Somehow excavating the depths of the human psyche will lead us to the same place, the same fear and loneliness."

Maya and Sarah completed each other. Every time Maya took off on flights of fancy, imagining that what she dreamed was real, Sarah came and brought her back down to earth, with her constant questions that gently shook Maya awake.

"Do you remember when I brought you a poster of Asmahan as a birthday gift? It was a little before you left for France. I didn't know that your passion would go further than hanging a poster up on your wall!"

"Of course I remember…. It's still hanging on the wall of my old room."

"Why Asmahan specifically? Who is going to read a book like this? Who is going to buy it?"

"I don't know. I haven't thought about that. I don't think that way. It is my passion. I don't know what I will produce. Sometimes I see what I am writing as a novel and not a biography. You understand this passion, Sarah! You have your own passion, you left everything to devote yourself to opening a café with a bookshop, you prepare light food and drinks, and you knew beforehand that you wouldn't make a profit off it! Who would go to a bookshop to drink a cup of coffee, tea, or a glass of something? But let's put this aside for a moment and go back to Asmahan. Did you know that she had a daughter, but they took her away by force? I wonder what she felt then. They denied her the right to motherhood. As if motherhood and art couldn't coexist. Perhaps she also believed that she didn't have the right to her own daughter. This will be the subject of the second chapter of my book."

"It is difficult to write a biography when at the same time you are calling what you are writing a novel.... No?" Sarah asked.

"Perhaps what I am doing will lead me to write first a biography, then a novel. I don't know. It's my first attempt. I will take it as far as I can. We will see together. What's confusing me now is that whenever I read more of Noura's diaries, I somehow feel that I share more things with her. There are bonds revealed every time I delve deeper into its pages. She writes against death through the story of her sister. Then she also writes about Yuri Gagarin. Part of it is because of her strange passion. I didn't know anything about him before now. It's as if she opened up my horizons and I found that they are connected to my life somehow. Don't ask me how. It is a vague feeling. Writing about lives cut short because of oppression. And then there's Gagarin and Asmahan.... Isn't that strange? They both died in shadowy circumstances, in tragic accidents. Both of them radiated out well beyond their own surroundings and more than was allowed to them. Asmahan's voice is enchanting, so is Gagarin's smile. I feel a certain sadness whenever I write about Asmahan. Is it her life or writing itself that makes me feel like this? Noura is right when she writes in her diaries, 'I started to feel despair writing about dying young people, but I came to realize that good writing begins with despair. It's the compass of writing—that's when we know that the blue hour, that moment between twilight and darkness, dawn and morning light, is near and that words are waiting to come out into the light.'"

Maya was reading nearly everything about Asmahan. She had started collecting everything that was published about her especially during the time when she worked with Bruno, the French director who asked her to research what Cairo was like during the first half of the twentieth century. When she started reading Noura's diaries she discovered that the family of this unknown woman, of whom there are no pictures, was from a village not far from the place where Asmahan spent her early childhood. The two of them are from the same culture and geographical region, Maya thought at the time.

Maya remembered Asmahan's voice ringing out at home, singing the song "Ya Tuyur," and her father sitting, head hanging over the edge of the high sofa, eyes closed, listening. Her mother, Aida, also loved Asmahan's voice, but she didn't sit or lean back on the sofa, or enjoy listening to her with her eyes closed, like her husband did. Aida used to move between the sitting room and the kitchen like a shuttle on a loom. Maya always felt that her mother never wanted her to see her father surrendering himself to a woman's voice like that, slowly abandoning the severity of his gaze as he listened with his whole heart. His severe gaze was his face's landmark and Aida never managed to make it softer or more tender in all the years they lived together. Her father listened, and Maya felt that Asmahan's voice tamed him, bringing him closer to her. Then a friend of his would come and sit near him, listening too. The women of the family were able to separate Asmahan's life from her voice with their words and actions. Maya reflected that a huge barrier had been erected from the time she was young. She and other young people had listened to Asmahan, true, but weren't allowed to talk about her. If they did want to, it had to be in the framework of pity, for Asmahan's lost morals, her failed motherhood, and her huge sins, which in the view of older women tarnished her reputation and led her toward perdition.

Maya finished writing the first chapter of *Asmahan* in Paris, before moving to Beirut. It was a working title; it was difficult to write without first having a title. She'd collected a huge amount of material, some of which contradicted what she'd read previously. Writing the history of an individual, she knew, not to mention a community, is a particular challenge, for it calls truth into question. Writers perhaps discover one day that they've used incorrect references because they based their writing on one "primary source," whose author cared less about serious research than making their own personal image shine brilliantly in history. Maya wondered if Asmahan's character was perhaps distorted in the articles published after her death. She didn't know and Asmahan couldn't come back to correct errors or defend herself. All Maya knew was that those published articles were to become the primary material for the authors of later books about the artist's life and death. *History sometimes becomes a lie and we have to face up to that lie and start from scratch in investigating and rewriting it,* thought Maya.

"I have to organize all the material I brought with me to Beirut that's piling up on my desk," Maya told Sarah while sitting on the sand. "But I can't do anything now. I have to finish the film first, then devote myself to writing about a woman who was killed at twenty-nine. Some say twenty-seven.... Then there's the book she was holding in her hand when she died. What was she reading, I wonder? The journalist doesn't mention the title, only that it was on her lap and she was wearing a yellow dress."

Maya said this while stretching out on the lukewarm sand, while Sarah sat on a chair and started reading Noura's diaries.

Shadi was playing near them, talking to himself, and Maya intentionally stayed close to the shore so her son could play in the sea. He started making a big sand castle. He scooped up water from the waves in a plastic pail and built wide walls for the moat around the castle. Then he started completely covering Maya with sand. When Sarah asked him what he was doing he said that he wanted to protect his mother from the heat of the sun.

Maya closed her eyes and let him play with the sand, putting it on her body. His response touched her deeply, and she thought of Zeyad. The heart remembers ... even if the body gets used to the separation.

A tingling in her back returned. It was a chronic pain she'd forgotten just as she'd forgotten her body. Maya thought she'd inherited her back and neck pains from her mother, who'd inherited them from her own mother. Perhaps the hot sand would soothe the pain, she told Sarah.

The sound of the unfinished movement of a wave intensifies, then fades. The rays of the sun warmed the sand that warmed her body. She was submerged within feelings of satisfaction and she thought that life might perhaps be gentler with her here in Beirut. But she just as quickly banished this thought from her mind when she was suddenly invaded by the fear of Zeyad's family taking Shadi away from her when he turned seven.

As if Sarah were reading her friend's fear at that moment, she closed the pages of the diary she was holding and asked, "Have you been calling Zeyad's family? Have they visited Shadi?"

"His uncle and aunt have come to Beirut twice. Then I didn't hear from the family after that. I will visit them when I have some time."

Sarah looked at her as if she were saying that she were lying, that she wouldn't visit Zeyad's family because she was afraid.

Maya closed her eyes again. The wave approached her and then receded, with Shadi continuing to cover the upper part of her body with sand. She must have dozed off for a moment. She started seeing thick, fiery clouds passing on the screen behind her closed eyes. She saw the metro she'd taken in Paris the day before she returned to Beirut and the man who threw himself under it—people's voices, sirens, the train stopping. Maya started screaming and running in every direction, running around in circles.

The clouds she could see with her eyes closed changed color. A bloody red covered this space and then suddenly disappeared, its place taken by a clear sky-blue. Eventually it turned dark gray, becoming diaphanous, like the smoke that came from Zeyad's cigarettes as he sat in front of an ashtray full of butts, near a bottle of wine. The three of them used to breathe in this smoke in their tiny flat in Paris. Every evening, Maya had to clean the place so it would be suitable for the baby to sleep there. Repeatedly she asked Zeyad to stop smoking in the apartment, to no avail. In the end, she would retreat to a little corner where she'd put a desk and a lamp so she could finish the first chapter of her Asmahan book, before hearing Zeyad asking her in protest to turn out the light.

Maya went to sleep and saw herself on the swing in the garden of her parents' summer house, her brother Nadim standing behind her, pushing the swing as she had asked him to. She started telling him, "More … harder…. That's not hard enough, not high enough, not fast enough…. More, do more!" But the swing stayed low.

Shadi came over to her and stretched out near her, then put his face close to hers and kissed her. She opened her eyes and looked at him smiling. He had Zeyad's eyes, but his skin was brownish like hers, and so was his hair. A small tear leaked out of the corner of her eye and dampened her cheek. She felt as though his kiss cleansed her soul of the pain stuck to it for so long. Her body started relaxing. Since she'd returned to Beirut, this was the first time Shadi had come close to her on his own without her insisting that he kiss her. Since they'd been back, he hadn't let her hug him as she loved to do. He used to cry in his bed; it wasn't exactly crying but something more like whimpering, as if a pain had woken him but soon weakened. She would rush from her room into his, come near his bed and sit on the edge, rubbing his shoulder and stroking his head so he would calm down and go back to sleep. Then she'd go back into her room and sleep.

She avoided sleeping next to him, though she wanted to. A stupid cultural norm that she'd grown up with always prevented her: a boy shouldn't be too attached to his mother, because of an absent father.... How many times had she heard stories of someone about whom people said, "He's a mama's boy" or "He's been raised by women." She also hesitated to move him to her bed, as if this would protect the illusion of a certain masculinity in her subconscious, a maleness that women stupidly reproduce with every son born to them, Maya thought.

Other times, she prevented herself from moving him into her bed simply because she felt that the left side of the bed was Zeyad's. Now it was empty, and she didn't want to fill the emptiness with her son.

As they drove back from the beach, Maya told Sarah that she really wanted to meet Kemal and she didn't know if she would find him. She told her that on her last visit to Sabah, she'd asked her about his address and Sabah had given her a little envelope in which she'd saved the picture of her disappeared husband, and on which Kemal had written his address and telephone number. Maya called this number many times but no one answered. Now she was thinking about putting his letters and Noura's diary in the big envelope and sending them to him.

But Maya's feelings were more complicated than whatever was causing her not to take a firm decision. She thought that it was the right of this man whom she'd never met before to read the diaries of the woman whom he'd loved and lost. But somewhere deep inside herself, she was scared of taking this step.

"What if he receives the envelope but doesn't come to Beirut to meet me as I hope? What if he's built a new life after all these years and he no longer cares about this? What if the envelope is delivered to someone in his family other than him and they throw it into the nearest wastepaper basket?" Sarah listened closely to Maya's questions while driving slowly on the road back to Beirut.

What Maya wanted most was to meet Kemal, to get to know him, to see his eyes and his hand, the hand that wrote those letters overflowing with love. She wanted to hear the voice that Noura's diaries described as caressing her. This description of ultimate love made Maya's heart miss a beat. "Do you want to meet him?" Sarah asked. "Then why send the diary and letters to him? Write him a letter! Ask to meet him in Beirut! You know what you want, no?"

Maya nodded without a word.

"So then, why are you betraying your own desires?" Sarah asked her excitedly.

"I really do betray my desires. I always delay responding to them, and I hate myself for that!" Maya replied.

"Sometimes fate is a lightning bolt," Sarah observed, "and strikes the core of your being, shaking it up. Death can be like that, but so can life and love. What's happened since you came back to Lebanon is exactly this bolt of lightning. Zeyad's death, first of all ... but those letters and diaries are a completely different kind of thing. They brought you back a certain equilibrium that you were missing. No doubt you wondered why it was you who found what you found in that demolished building? The lightning bolt didn't pass just like that. It changed your life. You won't ever be yourself again. You won't be who you were before, but a new woman."

Maya smiled and said, with a loving sarcasm her friend knew well, "Yes and what else.... Will I marry, travel, or stay here? You're like Fatima the fortuneteller my mother used to take me to visit when I was a child!"

The two friends laughed, and then Sarah said, "Be who you are, where you are. Every time I am confused or lacking confidence in what I'm doing, I repeat this to myself. It's my mantra."

The sun was setting slowly, breathtakingly, behind the horizon over the sea, accompanying them on their journey back to Beirut. Shadi was sitting in his seat, counting the number of shells he'd collected from the beach in Sour. Sarah pushed the button on the car's tape recorder to play a song. Maya let out a gratified sigh and the two of them started listening to Asmahan singing....

> When will you know, when ... that I love you....
> When will you know that I love you ... when,
> when, when...

Maya returned home with Shadi, putting him in the shower to wash the sand out of his hair and off his body. She used a loofa to scrub something that looked like black asphalt off his skin. Shadi started objecting to so much scrubbing especially on his legs, so she stopped. Then she sprayed him with warm water, which flowed all over his lean little body. She wrapped him in a white towel that Aida had brought when she visited them in Paris. It was a very large towel, which covered his body completely, the kind used in Turkish baths. She wished that her mother had brought another one too. She bought it in the Souq al-Hamidieh with spices for meghli and other things, which she'd carried to Paris in a separate bag.

Shadi was talking to Maya, who was half lost in thought. She didn't hear what he was saying to her as they entered his room and, exasperated, he repeated his request to go to the amusement park the following day; his auntie Nada had offered to take him while Maya was working. "Good, I will speak to Nada," she told him right away. She helped him put on his pajamas, and told him she would be back in a bit, asking him to get the story he would like her to read him. She went out onto the balcony and lit a cigarette. The front of her shirt was damp, and she felt a pleasant freshness on her breasts and belly. She liked this wet cold that protected her body from the evening's heat, even for a short time. The street was calm, unlike during the day. It was a brief opportunity for people to take refuge from the heat after the sun went down and before going out for the evening. The taste of smoke in her throat was dry and painful. Maya wanted something cold to drink in this heat, but there hadn't been electricity in the house since the early morning, when Israeli planes had bombed the power transformers. The city continually suffered from power cuts. The owner of the neighborhood generator was asking for double the amount to provide the additional hours of electricity. This was another expense Maya had not budgeted for. Life had become so expensive in Beirut. It was an absurd life; they were alive by chance, and living it was expensive. From the time she arrived from France, she lived with her mother in the family house. She felt that she had reverted to being a young girl and she didn't like it.

**

Maya thought about what Sarah had said to her, and she decided to send a few words to Kemal Firat by express mail, informing him of what she'd found in the suitcase and asking him if there was a possibility of meeting. She'd started to lose hope when a letter arrived three weeks later. She received an answer from Kemal Firat. He wrote that he would be visiting Lebanon at the end of November on a journalistic assignment. That was in two months, and if it were destined for them to meet at that time, they would meet. He was brief and distant in his letter; Maya had no way of knowing if her letter had brought him a bit of joy.

While waiting for her meeting with Kemal, she had to do many things. She had to finish the film. Then there was the book she'd started on Asmahan. Since she'd discovered the suitcase, she hadn't written even one word. The publisher was insisting she should finish it. She also had to transcribe everything she'd recorded during her last visit with Sabah. She had to move all that onto her computer as well as the notes she'd taken while reading Noura's diaries. None of this work was for the film—what she discovered took her further and further from the film each day, though it brought her closer and closer to herself. They were different worlds, different lives into which she let herself dive endlessly deeper. Passion took hold of her and led to where she'd never planned on going.

That evening Maya didn't want to stay home with no electricity. She would continue reading what remained of Noura's diaries the following weekend. The battery she normally used in her nightlight was totally dead. She felt like she needed to go out and have a drink at the café that Sarah had opened in Sodeco. She asked her mother to sleep in Shadi's room that night—at least until she got back. She said she wouldn't be late. Next week she would finish shooting the film with Danny.

12
NOVEMBER 1994

Maya was late waking up. She had to take Shadi to school to meet his new teacher, then go to meet Kemal Firat. It wasn't easy to find him, the author of the letters that she'd found in the bottom of an old suitcase in a damp attic of a semidemolished building in downtown Beirut. Even the thought of this meeting made her tense. What would he be like? Why did she want to meet him? Wasn't what she'd done up until now enough? When he'd called her from Jounieh, she couldn't believe it was him. He spoke to her in English with an odd-sounding accent. His voice was slow and neutral, fulfilling his duty to meet a woman who found letters and diaries from his past life. Maya put the phone down and thought she wouldn't go. She would call him at the hotel and cancel the appointment. But no! She told herself. She wanted to see him, to see the man who loved a woman so much despite the distance between their countries, with no regular phone connections or transportation in wartime.

She remembered Sarah's question at the beach, "How far will this passion take you, this passion that pushed you to meet a man whose letters, written eighteen years ago to a woman you don't know, whom you just happened to find?" *I don't know where this passion will lead me, just as I don't know why I want to know the end of the story,* thought Maya.

She wanted to hear the story from more than one person. Why wasn't what Sabah told her enough? And the letter and diaries, too? Wasn't all this enough? Did she want to follow the lives of people who were gone in order to recover their lives? Or did she want to expel the loneliness that had inhabited her since she'd last felt a man's touch?

An insistent need to reread parts of Kemal's letters to Noura inundated her, as if the letters were addressed to her. She also thought that if Noura had been there, she would have wanted to touch her. She smiled to herself. *Don't be stupid!* Then she started wondering what had happened to Kemal. How old was he now? He must be in his mid-fifties.

Those people whose traces she had found still had one fundamental thing in common: they loved and were passionate. They had the kind of passion that takes on many names. Maya clung to those people in order to capture a tempestuous love that she had never lived, a love that shakes your very being and uproots you, propelling you somewhere you never expected. She remembered what Sabah told her about her first relationship and running away from home: "It's not important how that love ended. What's important is that I loved. I tasted it. It was delicious, so delicious, Maya!"

It was a cloudy morning. Maya was thinking about all this while driving. She wondered what Noura looked like; she'd never seen a picture of her. She was the only one in this story who was strongly present but strongly absent at the same time. She had left a vibrant diary filled with love, passion, wisdom, questions, and life. She had collected texts, articles, and books on Yuri Gagarin, but she didn't have a face. Sabah talked about her only as a mind, as an intelligent and practical person. She didn't mention her face, hair, and eyes; Maya's questions didn't encourage her to speak about this. Maya could only try to picture Noura's face and body through Kemal's letters.

On the way to Jounieh, the sky darkened and the sun disappeared. The day transformed into a gray quasinight. It hadn't started raining yet that year, even though November was nearly at an end. There were new military checkpoints on the road, where cars were stopped and searched. The checkpoint of the Lebanese Forces in front of the Nahar al-Kalb tunnel had been removed following the arrest of the LF leader, al-Hakim Samir Geagea, along with a large group of others affiliated with the LF. Maya stopped to fill her tank, but she had to wait because of an electricity cut. Some young men standing near her were talking about al-Hakim and cursing both the Syrian regime and the Lebanese mukhabarat. One of them lowered his voice when a car pulled in and two men, one of them in military gear, went into the office at the back of the gas station.

It seemed to Maya that the area was living a silent time, fearing reprisals from groups affiliated with the security services that were collaborating with the Syrian Army in Lebanon.

She arrived near the hotel and parked the car in the lot. Heavy rain exploded suddenly, moments after she got out of the car, and it poured down shockingly hard. She didn't rush back to the car for shelter but kept walking instead, not taking refuge in a café before reaching the hotel. The sudden rain took her back to tender moments from her days as a student. She remembered Sarah laughing deeply when they would take cover in a café near the university.

Maya got to the hotel fifteen minutes before her appointment with Kemal. She looked like a drowned cat; humidity had penetrated her bones. The hotel was small and simple. She opted to wait for a few minutes to pass so her hair would dry a little. She sat on a sofa near the large window at the entrance. She started feeling increasingly cold. When she called Kemal Firat in his room, he said, "Come on up!" He said this simply, as if he knew her, or as if the idea of a woman going up to man's hotel room didn't mean anything to him. He just said with an innocent simplicity, "Come up, my room is number 422, on the fourth floor."

A hotel worker accompanied her to the elevator, pushed the button, and the two of them waited … but the elevator didn't come. The worker apologized, slightly sheepishly and stupidly, saying that perhaps the elevator was stuck on the top floor but he would go up and bring it down.

"No need," Maya replied. "I can go up the stairs." While hurrying up the stairs to the fourth floor, she thought to herself that in a country whose roads were still cut off and there were more military checkpoints than streets, of course hotel elevators were out of service.

Maya wasn't yet far up the stairs when she started panting. She stopped a bit to regain her breath. She didn't feel fine. She crossed the long corridor, which was covered with an orange-and-dark-blue striped rug, feeling her body tremble like a bird. She found the door to Kemal's room and felt sweat on the palm of her hand. Despite her wet hair, she felt heat emanating from her eyes. She couldn't see clearly yet. She hesitated before curling her fingers up and knocking. She didn't hear anyone coming to the door. She waited and then knocked again. The door opened slowly to reveal a man in his fifties, with mostly white hair that was thinning on top.

When he opened the door to her, Maya muttered something. Perhaps she said "Hello" or perhaps her name. A moment later she couldn't recall. But she felt that when their eyes met, the moment was unlike any before, that in some way she would be connected to what was to come. She stopped in front of the open door while Kemal invited her to come in, but he didn't move aside to make a space for her to walk through the door, as if something were holding him in place too and he'd lost the ability to move. He stayed there for a moment, standing, still, repeating, "Come in ... come in...."

The two of them spontaneously burst out in laughter, and only then did he move to the side so she could walk in.

"You're Maya, of course," he said with the hint of a smile on his face, his voice trailing off. "Of course," she replied. "Welcome," he said. She didn't need him to tell her that he was Kemal, and he didn't do so. If she'd seen him in the street, she'd have known him. She knew him from the photos, from the look in his eyes, the shape of his face, from how he stood. It was as if he hadn't changed. But there was something hardened in his gaze, created by years he had not yet forgiven—he was like someone who'd emerged from a lost war, not quite finding his way.

Maya didn't open the little bag she'd brought with her, inside of which were the photos, letters, and diary. He didn't give her the chance, either, because he started talking, as if he wanted to relieve himself of a heavy burden.

"You think I lost only Noura. No! I lost my whole life, and it was impossible to rebuild. We lose the one we love not only once, but many times in a row, over and over. It's a loss I feel even now, in this very moment, while telling you my story.

"I was imprisoned a few days before our son was born. I was on my way to Lebanon when the Syrian army arrested me and handed me over to Turkish security. Perhaps they'd made a deal, I don't know. Thus began a dark time in my life that lasted for five years. They arrested me, handcuffed me, and threw me in prison after charging me with plotting bombings and political assassinations in Turkey. The letters I wrote to Noura from prison weren't sent. I found this out only later. The security agency would read them and throw them in the trash. The charges against me were all fabricated. But my suffering in prison was nothing compared to the news that Taymour brought me that Noura and our son had been killed in a car bomb in Beirut. I no longer knew what to do. Did I even want to get out of prison? I had no more purpose in life—why should I leave? I thought it best to stay there, to rot away in a cell not even big enough for a bed. I am the one who failed to get her out of Beirut, when she asked me to, telling me that it had become too dangerous. I postponed getting her out, while waiting to organize documents so that we could travel all together to France.

"Hatred has a smell," Kemal continued after a pause. "It also has a rhythm. Noura smelled it and left Syria for Lebanon, but hatred followed her and killed her.

"Taymour wanted to inform Noura of my arrest, but he himself was also detained; he was imprisoned for seven months. When he got to Beirut, Sabah told him. At that point I knew everything. 'Tell Kemal that his family died, his wife and child, they both died. The war killed them in Beirut.' These were the last words she said to him before closing her apartment door.

"I was in prison for five years and got out by some unanticipated miracle. They'd sentenced me to ten years but for some reason I was released before the end of my term. Perhaps my French passport helped me. Putting a definitive end to my political work is the price I paid for my freedom, but what kind of freedom is that?

"When I got out, some people accused me of having squealed on my former comrades. During my last year in prison, the Turkish authorities mounted a campaign of arrests against a number of members of the Kurdistan Workers' Party, the PKK, including some of my comrades.

"The last time Noura and I met, she was almost ready to deliver. Her body remained graceful and her belly barely hinted at her pregnancy. I could see a gentle slope in total harmony with her taut body's natural slenderness. I will never forget that day … when we went to the Coral Beach pool in the afternoon. We walked a little toward the sea and Noura lay down on a towel she'd spread on the sand. She was exhausted from working nights as a journalist and wanted to sleep, even if for only five minutes.

"Looking at her stretched out on the sand with the sun disappearing over the horizon, painting its crisscrossed golden filaments over the roundness of her soft, feminine belly and the rest of her delicate body, I could never have thought that this would be the last time I'd see her. I didn't imagine that seeing her so exhausted and so profoundly distracted, both of which affected me deeply, would be something I would see with my own eyes once—one time in my life—never again to be repeated. When I looked at her, I felt that my heart was melting inside my chest and that nothing, nothing at all, could ever separate us, except death. And that's what happened. I didn't know that I would spend the rest of my life trying to recover both her presence at that moment and also those unique, complete feelings I had toward her.

"When I returned to Lebanon for the first time after the death of Noura and our child, Sabah took me to Bashoura Cemetery, to the place where she'd wanted to bury her husband if they'd returned his corpse to her. She stood near an empty space covered with dry grass and scattered stones, pointed to a dusty, neglected corner, and told me that Noura and the baby were buried there. I don't know what happened to me. Nightmarish moments. I couldn't believe it. It was as if Noura had passed on just the day before, as if we had been together only moments earlier.

"I couldn't stay more that two days. Beirut seemed hard-hearted, unwelcoming, incomplete. Places took on different meanings; only then did I see how strange and lonely the city was. How could I start my morning when every street and café reminded me of her? How could I pick myself up? With her gone, I was no longer a man.

"I left the next morning and didn't return to Beirut again after this, though I'd put in a request to the director of my news agency in Istanbul to be transferred there. If she were still alive now she would be forty-six years old, our son would be seventeen, and we would be a family nourished by love, believing that there is a tomorrow.

"We all have our black holes—she used to tell me this. I now understand what she meant. Here I am now in the deepest black hole of loneliness.

"I left prison and felt alienated. It was only five years but that was enough for me to see that the world had changed. The world had no more heroes. With ash-filled mouths and wounded souls, my only remaining comrades looked like they'd aged decades. I felt that from now on we would no longer catch the butterflies of our dreams; surely we've had enough crying and are too busy with the blisters on our hearts, which need a lifetime to heal."

Maya listened to Kemal as though devouring his words. He would stop speaking for a moment and then start up once more. It was the passion she'd been searching for her entire life, but never found. She felt it now and she would feel it tomorrow. Did she find it because of the power of his words, or the power of the love that still pulsated inside him? It was a love buried with a dead woman whom she'd never seen.

Kemal would sometimes stop speaking and ask a question, as if he wanted to be sure that Maya was following what he was saying. She was following him silently, with a silence that birthed a deep bond between them in a way that words could not. In one of these moments it occurred to her to throw down one sentence, just like that, in one burst, like a gambler throws dice on backgammon board: "Your letters changed something inside me."

When she bade him farewell, it was still raining outside, as if the rain would accompany Kemal's story to the end. Maya didn't feel that she had already spent almost half a day with him. She wanted to sum up an entire lifetime on that autumn day with Kemal. Perhaps because she felt that a long time had passed by uselessly, and that the two of them had to drink in this entire lifetime like coffee in the morning.

She went back to Beirut at the beginning of the evening, rain hitting her windscreen forcefully. The wipers didn't work very well and she had to drive slowly. Maya got home and was shivering. The first thing she did was make tea. She didn't wait for it to cool down even slightly; she drank it and burnt her tongue and the roof of her mouth. She held her mug of tea in both her hands to warm up. The sound of the rain mixed with Kemal's words, which were still ringing in her ears.

She went back again to Kemal and Noura's letters, and reread some of them despite being exhausted and sleepy. The letters had taken on a different flavor.

Then Maya wrote in her notebook:

Kemal,

I will write about you late at night before I sleep. I read your letters that never reached me. A woman read them before me. I found them years later. How could I have been unaware of this all my life? I found all of that love here, all of the love I lost long ago.

**

Maya was exhausted and sleepy. She went into Shadi's room, lay down next to him in bed, held him in her arms, and quickly fell asleep.

13

THE LAST PAGES OF NOURA'S DIARY

Maya's heart always opened at a certain point before she reached Bourj al-Murr on foot. A little spot near the Holiday Inn, through which one could suddenly see the horizon expand and an intensification of blue. *Beirut is a giant construction site*, she thought to herself. *The noise of renovation dominates the sounds of the sea, people, church bells, and the azaan. They build and dump out at the same time. They dump violence out as if it weren't there. They dump violence out with even greater violence. But it's still there and will come back from under the ground, even from the heart of the sea itself.* Maya continued her walk downward, passing in front of the Phoenicia Hotel, which was also mired in endless renovation. She crossed the road and walked toward Manara. Semidestroyed buildings were confiscated and made into barracks by the Syrian Army. Women and men walked for exercise along the seafront sidewalk. Maya stopped a moment to rest, leaning her body against the green iron railing. Across from her, a young woman wearing a long blue satin shirt over white trousers sat on a stone bench, also watching the passersby, but cautiously and with a bit of fear. She had a suitcase with little rolling wheels. She passed her hand over her belly in little circles, slowly and cautiously, as if she were consumed by something that preoccupied her. She raised her hand to her hair and pushed it out of her face. Then she put her hand on her forehead and leaned her body forward as if she were staring at something specific on the ground. But it seemed as if she were thinking about something that was worrying her. Sadness on this young woman's face drew Maya to her. She looked at Maya with a half smile, and Maya initiated a warm greeting without words. The young woman returned the greeting, her lips shaped in a slight, fleeting smile. Then she turned her head gracefully, pushing her hair back once again, and went back to watching the people passing by in front of her as if she were waiting for someone or looking for a particular face. At a certain moment, she held her cell phone up to her ear, said a few words, and then put it back in her bag. Her eye quivered as if a tear were waiting to fall. God seemed to have abandoned her at that moment.

Maya kept walking toward the Bain Militaire, then crossed over to get to Rawda Café. She sat near the cement walls facing the sea. It was a sunny and warm Beirut October day. Women of all shapes and ages, their faces intermingled with argileh and cigarette smoke, wearing short dresses, flowing trousers, and hijabs. Flowing fabrics pulled over bodies, all colors—pastels, bolds, and black. Fabric waved over bodies that the years had exhausted. The owners of these bodies wanted to cover up their fatigue, and take refuge under God's tent.

Maya drank a cup of coffee and then took out the notebook filled with Noura's diaries to read the final pages:

[...]

A call from my father this morning. The short story I wrote about my sister Henaa that was published in an Arabic magazine in London reached them. "We want you here," he told me. "You must deny this story and get a retraction published in which you make it clear that someone was impersonating you. You're crazy, you don't know the consequences of what you've done."

My father's call was brief, a reprimand. He didn't ask me one question about my health or work. I didn't tell him anything either. No one even knew about my marriage since I'd started receiving threats.

[...]

Since my story about Henaa was published and my father and brother's phone calls, as well as Huda's ... they haven't stopped. They're threats, not communication. At first, I didn't believe what they were saying on the phone. I believed that they were my family's intimidation to regulate my behavior and prevent me from continuing to write stories that affected them. My father said that I was doing something that would destroy the family. Am I destroying the family because I told the truth? Because I simply wrote what happened? Families prefer silence, always silence. But silence doesn't stop death or suicide and it doesn't prevent women from killing themselves. Didn't Henaa's suicide destroy the family too? Why does everyone hold Henaa responsible? They hold the dead person responsible for her own death! Huda told me, "Why did your sister agree to this relationship? She's responsible." Everyone shirks the responsibility of their silence, as if they were killing Henaa once again.

I can't forget her sobs the night before she killed herself. The doors were closed right in her face but I didn't understand that then. They said that my mistake was that I published the story with real names, that someone gave a copy of the magazine to Shawqi and that he lost his mind when he read it, threating to send my father back to prison and to get my brother fired from his job. He said that a story like this would destroy his future and everything he had achieved. But it won't affect his future—perhaps it will even help him, since the requirements for promotion in the security services all begin with criminal activity. I also know that I wouldn't be free from his evil even if he were to carry out all his threats against my father and brother. He has spread rumors that I was working for the British secret services. How could a journalist outside Syria not working for the regime's media outlets and not praising the regime *not* be accused of being an agent? If that journalist were a woman, then she'll not only be accused of being an agent, but also of being a whore! Huda repeatedly asked me for Henaa's letter. But there's no use in sending the letter now, and there's no use ripping it up here. It's too late in any case.

[...]

I am writing to myself. I am writing to Kemal as well. Perhaps it is my only way to feel close to him and stay distant from him, too. This is not an easy equation to control, as if it's on the verge of being permanently uncontrollable and that's what gives it meaning, but for now I'm going to put talking about meaning to one side. I think that this notebook of mine will serve as letters to him that will be deferred until we meet. In our last phone call, I told him that I wanted to leave Beirut and that it would be better to do so before our baby is born. But where to go? It's the first time I asked him this. It is the first time that

I've had fear in my heart and lost my feeling of safety.

July 1978

I knew that Kamal sneaking into Beirut from Izmir would be difficult and I would see our son for the first time all by myself. I went into the hospital at dawn yesterday and our son was born at two in the afternoon.

On the way to the hospital I said to myself, "Sometimes doctors make mistakes." After my son was born I dozed off, weakened from the fatigue. Between sleep and waking I heard the obstetrician's voice saying it was a boy. But the idea that a beautiful girl had come out of my body stuck in my mind. I thought at the time that he was joking with me.

It was a hot day; the air conditioning in the delivery room wasn't working. At that moment I felt that hell wasn't far from Beirut. [...]

That evening I asked for a delicious dinner and a glass of wine. The dinner came without the glass of wine. "Hospital rules," said the nurse. I laughed and told her, "Next time I'll give birth in a bar, at least they'll bring me a drink!"

Despite Kemal not being there during

the birth or even in Beirut, I felt a strong desire for life and laughter that evening.

[...]

Right now, I'm in my hospital room reading what Kemal wrote me in his last letters. He nourishes hope wherever he is. We really need big doses of it from him! I will try to nurture hope here as well, despite the violence all around us, I tell myself while my fingers hold the hand of my little one, born yesterday.

**

Karim (let's make this his temporary name) sleeps all day. Sometimes I have to wake him up to breastfeed him. As soon as he finishes, he falls back asleep again.

**

A *Breath of Life* is the title of a book I received today as a gift from a woman colleague of mine.

On one of its pages, the author, Clarice Lispector, says, "I write as if to save somebody's life. Probably my own."

I read her words ravenously while Karim was devouring my breast, hurting my nipple. It's as if she were writing about me.

12 August 1978

I don't know what has come over me since early this morning. Is it the postpartum depression I've read about? Karim has been crying; my breast milk isn't enough for him. A certain anxiety takes hold of me … actually it's fear.

Tomorrow is my appointment at the embassy. I won't wait for Kemal. I called his office after he didn't answer his personal telephone. They said he hasn't come to work for more than two weeks. I'm waiting for him and don't know anything about what's happened to him.

13 August 1978

I handed Karim to Sabah. As she took him from my arms, it was as if he were being ripped out of my heart. I will come back from the embassy in the afternoon to bring him home and organize everything I've collected about Yuri Gagarin. The time for my book about him has come.

My boss can go to hell.

Maya stopped reading the last pages of Noura's diary, stunned. What Noura wrote about the last two days before she was killed was a surprise. The baby wasn't with her when she went to the embassy!

This was extremely strange. Maya had to know what had really happened to the baby. She remembered her last meeting with Sabah and Sabah's nervousness when Maya asked her about the picture of her with the baby. At that time, Sabah didn't want to talk at all about Noura's son, and she started asking her own questions—perhaps so Maya would forget her question and not wait for an answer. Maya quickly put the notebook with the diary and the scattered papers back into her bag, and left Rawda Café. She walked on the sidewalk across from the wall of the Bain Militaire toward Ain el Mreisseh. A big fuss rang out, the sounds of ambulances and police, drowning out all other sounds. No sooner did Maya walk near the place where she had stopped and leaned against the wall leading to the café, than these sounds increased. Cars, loud noises, and people standing around in a circle, in the center of which a corpse was laid out on the ground while the civil defense staff covered it with a sheet.

Maya was able to see part of the clothes the corpse had on: a blue satin shirt and wide white trousers clearly showed through the short cover pulled over her face and part of her chest. Maya screamed, "That's her ... her ... her." A policeman came over to her and asked, "Do you know her?"

"Yes ... yes ... Well, no ... no ... I mean I saw her today for the first time and we exchanged friendly glances." Maya started crying as if she had known the victim for some time. "It was an honor killing," someone told her. "One of her family members killed her and turned himself in to the police." Was she also a migrant? Maya asked herself. Was she running away or was she compelled to come here as happened to Sabah, to Noura, and to Mala, all migrants who left their countries because of a man or a family of men? Maya tried to walk but she felt herself collapsing. She sat on a stone bench and burst into tears.

Some time passed before she started walking on the road from Spears Street toward Ayoub Station, as the voices of the muezzins rang out in the air from more than one direction. The cars lessened in number and then disappeared. It was time for Friday prayers. A kind of calm reigned in the streets. Stray dogs on the corner flocked to food thrown at them. Remains of human waste were scattered on the sidewalk, and the smell of urine lingered in the air. Maya walked slowly up the road, as she felt anxious about appearing rushed. A car slowed down while passing her, and the man in the passenger seat pelted her with an empty pack of cigarettes, verbally harassing her. The pack hit her shoulder and landed on the sidewalk. The driver slowed even more, giving his companion a chance to leer at her. Maya bent over, grabbed the empty pack, and flung it as hard and as angrily as she could back at the man's face, shouting and almost crying, "Throw it in your trash at home.... You're all the same, you're all murderers!"

"God save us from this tigress!" called out the man, leaning his head out the car window. "What kind of a tigress is this?" He kept repeating this before finally saying to the driver, who sped off, "God save us! She's a madwoman."

God save us? thought Maya angrily. *What "god" is this jerk talking about? Why is it that whenever the number of pious people* goes up, the number of murders of women goes up? Then Maya started repeating what she'd heard, but as a question: "God save us?"

She got home exhausted. She was unsettled and didn't know what to do. She sat on the sofa and leaned her head forward, resting it between the palms of her hands. The sight of that woman's corpse lying on the ground—it was the same woman who'd smiled at her a few hours before, and then everything suddenly just stopped. They'd exchanged greetings; it was as if they'd spoken, though Maya didn't even know what the murdered woman's voice had sounded like.

These were difficult days for Maya. Her life had gone through tumultuous changes—and then came the suitcase, people whose destinies the war had changed, a war that had shattered their stories. And, now, on this day, all this violence. The violence of war and the violence of peace were two sides of one reality, neither of which she knew how to deal with well. Maya went back to reading the final pages of Noura's diary, which said that her child wasn't with her when she went out. But did that even make sense? She couldn't believe what she was reading.

Her discovery that baby Karim wasn't with his mother on the day of her murder made Maya anxious. Nonstop questions ran through her mind. If the baby had stayed with Sabah, then where was he? Why did she say he was killed? Did Noura change her mind at the last minute and take her son with her? But the last words in her diary were, "I handed Karim to Sabah," and then also, "I will come back from the embassy in the afternoon to bring him home." This meant that she gave

Karim to Sabah and then went back to her apartment before going to the embassy. If not, how was she able to write those final words?

Maya woke in the early morning hours to find she'd been asleep on the sofa with her clothes and shoes still on, and that the electricity had come back on, so the lights were now on in almost all the rooms of the apartment.

She got into her bed, taking Noura's diary with her, but couldn't get back to sleep until 4 AM. Maya didn't know out of which Pandora's box her nightmares came during this short period of sleep. She saw Zeyad lying there, his eyes open. She didn't cry; she remained calm, as if she knew she were having a nightmare. "We must close his eyes," she said. "It's our duty to close the eyes of the dead, because if their eyes remain open, they stay in that place between heaven and hell." But Maya didn't believe in heaven and hell. She came close to him and stretched out her hand to close his eyes, which were staring at her, cold and fixed.

Weeks before he died, Zeyad told her that never in his whole life had he been a believer, that he used to make fun of the holy books and religious people.

"Now that I am at death's door, what if it turns out all that all those lies are true? Maya don't you sometimes wonder what there is on the other side of life, what there is after death?"

**

In the morning, Maya dropped Shadi off at school. He didn't want to go, because it was a new place. It was much bigger than his daycare. He wanted to stay with her. Her being preoccupied and distracted perhaps also made him feel less secure. Maya parked the car near the school. She thought that this would be the best way to get back more quickly in the afternoon to pick him up. It can be much faster to move around on foot in Beirut because of the traffic. She had to get to the hotel to ask about Kemal. She was afraid that there might be some emergency that would force him to rush back to Turkey. She couldn't even wait until their upcoming appointment—she had to see him then.

14
THE PAST RETURNS

From the day she handed the child over to Adèle al-Naa'es at the end of 1978, Sabah wanted to forget. She wanted to throw memory in the bottom of a well, never to return. But it did return.

The past returns.... It returns, coming in the house, sleeping in the bed, putting everything we hate on our pillow. How can we sleep, then?

Noura entrusted Sabah with her son on the day she went to register him at the Turkish embassy. But Noura didn't come back to pick up her son. Sabah waited for an hour, two hours, many hours for her to come back. When she learned that there had been an explosion, night had already fallen. At the beginning, she didn't believe it. She started circling the house, carrying the little baby, telling herself that the news couldn't be true, that the embassy was far away from where the bomb went off, and wondering where Noura had been all day, since the embassy closed at three in the afternoon.

What is she doing? Sabah thought to herself angrily, *She dies and disrupts my life, leaving me a month-old baby I don't know what to do with.*

Then her anger lifted, as she suddenly realized that Noura had died. *Not one more time, please God. She's my family, I don't have any family other than her.* Sabah sobbed, looking at the baby's face, talking to him. As if Noura could intuit her own death, she used to tell Sabah, "I am afraid of forgetfulness. I am afraid that when he comes I will have forgotten what I did. Writing in my diary is my memory."

Sabah used to believe that she knew Noura completely. She knew her when they talked. And when Noura walked over and put her hand on her shoulder, Sabah noticed how tall she was and felt that the two of them had lived a previous life together. But at certain moments, Sabah's feeling that she knew this woman dissipated—especially during Noura's long telephone conversations with Kemal. When what she was saying was somewhat strange, Sabah didn't understand anything. In some way she transformed into another woman or perhaps into many women. It's possible that Sabah only knew one of these women, and believed it was impossible to equate them. She had never seen her so afraid and nervous as she was that last morning. News from Taymour stopped after his last visit, and Sabah heard that he was murdered in 1979; Turkish forces killed him during the hunt for members of the PKK, the new party that he'd help found. At the time, Taymour's death seemed to Sabah like another confirmation that she was doing what was right, in giving the baby to Adèle al-Naa'es to ensure a happy life for Karim in a European family that wanted to adopt him. *If the baby had stayed here, what would I have done after Taymour's death? What would I have done with a little baby, when I couldn't even support myself?*

Then Sabah started repeating the same questions to convince herself, once again, that what she was doing was the best solution.

What would my husband Ahmad say if he came home and saw me holding a little baby? How would he believe that it was not my son and that I hadn't gotten pregnant and given birth to another man's child?

When Kemal visited her for the first time after Noura's death, more than five years had passed. That's when he confirmed Taymour's death to her. Sabah accompanied him to the nearby cemetery where many unidentified bodies were buried. She pointed to a spot. Kemal returned to Turkey and once or twice sent Sabah money. He gave her his address and telephone number in case she needed anything.

Noura passed away, but Sabah remembered her every time she stood inside the kiosk ringing up customers, writing down orders. She remembered her whenever she went back to her apartment to do the evening's sales inventory. Were it not for Noura, Sabah would never have learned accounting or even to write her name next to some of the words.

Sabah opened her little kiosk after she gave away the baby, and started selling bottles of water and mana'eesh, which she initially baked on her own. The neighborhood gunmen were her clients, buying her mana'eesh. Then they started asking her to stock cigarettes and alcohol for them, too. Sabah started selling them just about everything. If any one of them tried to come near her, she used to transform into a fierce tigress; she didn't know how she succeeded in convincing them to leave her and her business alone. Perhaps it was because she stayed in the neighborhood and didn't leave, or perhaps it was because the mothers of those young fighters knew her. She used to drink coffee with these women and read the grounds at the bottom of their coffee cups, informing them of their daughters' weddings and letters that would arrive with money and gifts enclosed. Other times Sabah told them stories about the neighborhood's original inhabitants, who'd fled at the beginning of the war, leaving their apartments and furniture in their homes, even leaving chandeliers hanging from the ceilings still lit. In the eyes of the new residents, Sabah became the building's memory, preserving both its secrets and those of the old neighborhood—past and present. For her, the feelings these secrets evoked were contradictory, somewhere between love and fear, competition and hatred. When the building's new residents fought about something—especially about the drinking water, which barely reached all the way to the top floor, or about where to keep their garbage while waiting to take it away to be burned after the municipality's public trash collection ceased—then they would remind her that she was Kurdish, a foreigner, and they were the locals!

Sabah wouldn't answer. Instead she would wait for the right opportunity to say what was in her heart: "I am Lebanese, my husband Ahmad is Lebanese. My father's sister has been Lebanese for a long time. That damned woman succeeded in getting Lebanese nationality back in President Chamoun's days." She would say this to the women while reading coffee grounds.

"Over my dead body," Sabah used to say in the early years of the war, when one of the fighters would flirt with her, starting to tease her by reaching out to grope her breasts. "Over my dead body," she would repeat, pushing his hand off her, then add, "I could be your mother, boy." Actually not that many years separated Sabah from the fighters, perhaps only a few, but she became old before her time.

In the beginning, Sabah didn't let any one of them come near her. Had the man she loved and had lived with for twenty days died? She used to tell herself that he, following his abduction, he was living somewhere unknown. But, after some time, she did let the young fighters come closer and closer to her. Sabah let them have her body, which had grown tired of waiting. She would close her eyes, and while one of them had sex with her, she would try to recall the four nights in Istanbul with her boyfriend Ahmed. But she would fail every time. She opened her eyes and all that was in front of her was a coarse face, the fetid smell of sweat, and military fatigues in a pile on the floor.

Did she let them invade her life, mind, and body because of Noura's death? Or because of her terrible feelings of guilt for giving up Karim? Or because of her own vulnerability, which only increased during the war years and that she could no longer contain?

Sabah let them come and go from her home on the ground floor of the building. Sometimes they would climb over the partially destroyed wall and jump into the apartment's back garden, coming in through the narrow kitchen door, which didn't have a lock. She let them have her body. If one of them were on top of her, constricting her ability to breathe for a few minutes, Noura's voice and the baby's face when Adèle al-Naa'es took him and left would at times flash before her. Sabah hated herself in those moments; she hated the kiosk that she rented with the little money she got from Adèle. She didn't want to think; she didn't want to remember. She no longer told the fighters, "You'll only have me over my dead body." They did have her. And then came a profound feeling that parts of her body were dying. It started start deep inside her, then moved to her breasts, belly, and genitals. She kept waiting for her disappeared husband. She became a dead body waiting for a dead body. One of them brought her news about her husband, swearing he'd seen him—they'd been cellmates in an underground prison in East Beirut. She believed him and started making inquiries. He started coming and going to her place all the time and she started crying on his shoulder. Then, after some weeks, he spoke to her crankily, "Don't cry over your husband every time we want to do it with you!" After that he got up, put on his clothes to go out, and was gone for a long time.

Despite this, somewhere in her traumatized soul, some of Sabah's pride still remained. She repeated to herself, "She did what she did for herself, by herself, thanks to no one." No thanks to her father, who sent her letters asking for money under the pretext that he would save it for her. No thanks to her brother, who had failed in both school and work. No thanks to her husband, who had disappeared in the war and whose name was the loveliest thing about him. With the money that she sent to her family in Turkey, her father bought a little apartment for her brother in the outskirts of Istanbul. He left his wife—Sabah's mother, who was afflicted by Alzheimer's—to slowly stifle in their old house in the mountains of Mardin. After all the money Sabah had sent him, he didn't save anything at all for her, his daughter, to have for herself when she went home. Why would he? For him, she was a just woman at the end of the day. And she was not merely a woman, but a woman not in Mardin, who, more-over, didn't have a man. These two reasons were enough in the eyes of the men of the family for Sabah to be considered practically dead.

Right in the middle of the war, Sabah used to feel safe from death. The war happened outside her house like a game. She made mana'eesh and tea for the heroes of this game every morning. She didn't fear anyone. She saw them as heroes in a game called "The War" and she didn't see them as men. *I don't have men here in Beirut,* Sabah thought. She'd been waiting for her husband Ahmad for a long time. She was waiting because she wanted to know what happened to him, because she didn't want to finish her life in this way, "neither in or out," as she said. And also because she was on the edge of an abyss, in all ways, the first of which was madness. She sometimes thought about death, but she didn't dare go there willingly. So too, she was getting older, and this frightened her. Nonetheless, Sabah would sometimes still wake up with the delightful feeling that she was still in her twenties and that time was waiting for her—along with Germany, where her boyfriend Ahmad was. But those morning thoughts quickly dissipated when she found it difficult to get out of bed because of the pain in her back, which had afflicted her ever since Shawqi the army officer attacked her, pushing her down six flights of stairs in Noura's building. Sabah's treacherous, cursed body insisted on reminding her of the past, of incidents she wanted to forget. Then she remembered her mother in Mardin, who used to always say, "Akh ... Akh," as though it were a part of inhaling and exhaling.

But what she recalled most in the dawn hours, when still in bed, were the faces of those women who used to gather under the Mardin morning sun to talk about their aches and pains and how life passes by so quickly. An image of many old women, from her mother's mother to her father's mother to her father's aunt to their elderly neighbor. They sat on the edge of the road near the house, located between the front terrace and the village graves, scattered throughout a large rectangular area filled with cypress, oak, and olive trees, all trees that keep their leaves year round. As a pre-adolescent, Sabah believed that those trees stayed green through autumn and beyond to shade the souls of the dead in their graves.

The village lost its men for most of the year. They left for cities to do wage labor, leaving the women and children at home. They came back at the end of each season for two or three days, then left again, coming back to celebrate the birth of a new child in the family. Later, they started returning less frequently and sometimes they didn't return at all during the year. Sabah's grandmother, who also carried her name, sat with her hands in her lap staring silently into the distance.

From far away, she and the other women looked like replicas of Penelope: women waiting for men to come back from work, for fighters to come back from war. The war comes and goes, and they keep waiting, dressed in somber clothes. Sabah's mother said that this was the thing that scared her the most when she first entered her husband's family home after just turning thirteen. She saw the elderly women in their long dark dresses. One of them, Sabah's maternal grandmother, wore ample, colorful skirts that she sewed by hand from fabric she'd found here and there. She was said to have come from nearer to the city, where colorful clothes were preferred. Some of the old women carried strings of blue prayer beads that protected them from the evil eye. They slid the beads along the string, and the only sounds to be heard were the clicking of beads and the starlings in the tree branches around the graves. One of the women broke the silence at times to say, "When a day passes, it will never return again." Then another would follow: "Only a little bit of life is left, no one can live out someone else's years." The old women's voices would rise up in assorted, dissonant rhythms, repeating what was said like a mantra. Then they would sigh. A long silence would follow their sighs.

On her last visit to Mardin, Sabah saw her Alzheimer's afflicted mother looking right at her and smiling. The harsh woman who had so frightened her and her brother was no more. She looked at Sabah, who'd dyed her hair a bright golden color; she reached out to her daughter while inhaling like a child. "The sun has fallen on her shoulders!" exclaimed Sabah's mother with a dull, flaccid laugh. Then she was silent and stared off into space. She called her husband Baba, and asked him to buy her candies when he went out. Then, a few minutes later, she'd ask him where he was going. Sabah hugged her for a long time before she went back to Beirut. She knew it would be their final goodbye.

15
A HEART CALLED FEAR

Maya called the hotel and found that Kemal had already left for the airport. She knew that he would be back in three weeks. But she couldn't wait, so she went alone to confront Sabah.

Sabah was lying on the sofa when she heard a knock at the door. When she saw that Maya was there without having called first, it was as if she'd expected this visit. Perhaps it was time to talk, Sabah thought, time to say everything—not thanks to her courage but because she was in the depths of fear. Fear was not unknown to her anymore. For years she'd been in the grips of an anxiety that ate away at her soul every night. She definitely expected Maya's anger and her questions. Why didn't she tell Taymour the truth when he visited her? Why didn't she tell Kemal five years after Noura's murder? How could she not have told him that his son Karim hadn't been killed, that in fact he was still alive somewhere on this planet? How?

Maya asked her all this angrily, but she was paralyzed by helplessness. Questions about why, one question after another, followed by short words: how, when, where.

Sabah knew that any response would only be an occasion for Maya to ask more questions, to doubt her. Even Sabah didn't understand how this had all happened. How had she given the baby to Adèle al-Naa'es? After she did so, she started to fight with her memories. She hated them, butted up against them every night, closing her eyes and squeezing them tightly to maybe sleep. After Noura died and she gave away the baby, the war years seemed like a blessing to Sabah, even with bombardments that shook the building. It was that daily bloodshed around her which at the time made her imagine that her memory of what she had done would remain safely far away. But after not too long, torment ate slowly away at her soul. "The baby is in a safe place," she used to tell herself, a cloud of cigarette smoke blocking the television screen, which was announcing a new ceasefire. "The baby is in a safe place," she repeated on lonely nights, looking at the gaping mouths of military boots on the floor, waiting for some fighter to finish and get off her silenced body, stretched out on the mattress. She'd lost all feeling in her body. "Were it not for a forgetfulness that embraces our buried sins, we would have thrown ourselves off the rooftops of Beirut's buildings to be free of the heaviness of the past," she would whisper to herself after the man left her house. She let cold water flow from the rubber hose over her pudendum and vagina, touching them with her soapy hand.

But was it really forgetfulness or something else, something resembling a slow death?

When Maya asked her how she could abandon the baby, the fruit of two people's love, Sabah answered, angrily, "Love? Where was Karim supposed to find love? At his grandfather's house? With Noura's family? If the child had remained here, he'd have been nourished only on hatred. He would have only experienced treachery and death."

"Have you no heart?" Maya asked her dryly.

"Indeed I do have a heart," Sabah shot back. "It is called fear!"

The snippets of stories that Maya heard from Sabah in their previous meetings were only a small part of a larger story, which Noura had left behind in the final pages of her diary.

After she first met Noura, Sabah was very happy; she used to walk up from Khandaq al-Ghamiq to Zeidaniya to take care of the apartment and prepare food whenever she was away. After Noura met Kemal, the two of them were Sabah's family in Beirut.

Sabah was tense that day Noura entrusted her baby to her. Noura told her that she hadn't slept well the night before and that she was afraid—perhaps she foresaw her own death. She transferred this fear to Sabah. She walked to the door, then came back and kissed Karim. She stood there for a few minutes, and then asked Sabah to go to her flat at some point during the day and get her things, the baby's things, and her papers. On that day Sabah didn't think that Noura could know fear. But for an unclear reason, on that day, perhaps a fear she'd felt for the first time only then, Noura didn't want to go back to her flat in Zeidaniya.

While Karim was taking his nap that day, Sabah asked Mariam to stay at her place while she went to Noura's apartment to collect everything she and the baby would need. As if Noura's fear had been transferred onto her, Sabah got all Noura's papers together and put them in a suitcase. They included Kemal's letters, a notebook containing her diaries, photos, official documents, miscellaneous personal papers, and the entire archive Noura had assembled about Yuri Gagarin. She spun around the flat, looking for papers and stories on the shelves and in the desk drawers and cupboards. She couldn't forget what Noura had once told her: "If they knew what I was writing they would drag me through the streets, Sabah." Sabah remembered Noura saying this, and so she threw every piece of paper she touched into the plastic bag she'd brought with her. She carried all of these papers and notebooks back home and waited for Noura to come back from the embassy. After she learned about Noura's murder, Sabah put everything belonging to Noura in a special leather suitcase, and waited for Kemal—or someone he'd send from Turkey—to come and take it, along with the child who was left behind. But Sabah heard nothing from him.

When she moved to Ibrahim's apartment for fear of the mukhabarat officer, she took the suitcase with her and added it to her own things, in particular, pictures of herself and of her disappeared husband. Ibrahim, who had lost his wife and child, grew used to the baby and loved him. Sabah started sharing her food with the baby and buying him milk and the other things he needed. She also looked after Mariam and regularly went to the pharmacy to get her rheumatism medication. Most of the residents of her own building had left, anyway, and displaced families had come and occupied the empty apartments, so Sabah couldn't work there as she had before. The new, migrant families didn't hire her to clean their houses, and no one paid the caretaker's salary anymore.

Sabah waited every day for six months for a letter to come, a letter that would tell her what to do with the child, who wasn't her flesh and blood, but whom she suddenly found in her care the day his mother was murdered. No one from Noura's immediate or extended family came—those people she avoided and hid from, especially her cousin's husband the mukhabarat officer. The baby stayed with Sabah for six months, when her friend Mariam told her that a woman called Adèle al-Naa'es wanted to help her.

"Over there, Karim will be raised in the sort of affluence you can't possibly provide him with," the woman who visited her with her husband, George Shammas, assured her. "He'll go to school, eat, and have clothes; he'll have a mother and father like other children."

Sabah hesitated to accept. She told herself, *Perhaps he's a gift I've been given because I haven't yet been blessed with a child. Perhaps God put him in my lap to compensate me for my lack of someone to love in my life. But how can I keep him far from that officer? How will I protect him from that monster? How will I get him what he needs? How will I educate him? How will I pay his medical bills? How will I keep him from joining the fighters when he is older? How will I stop him from becoming a murderer like them?*

Concerns and questions plagued her like the devil. When Adèle returned after a few weeks with Mariam, Sabah accepted her offer. The woman took the child and flew to Europe. Sabah heard nothing after that, no news from either her or her husband.

After the child left, Sabah returned to Khandaq al-Ghamiq. There, Taymour visited her to tell her Kemal was in prison. The Turkish forces had arrested him because of his political activism, accusing him of planning bombings in Izmir. He also informed her that Kemal had sent many letters to Noura but he'd not received a thing from her. Sabah told Taymour about the car bomb and Noura's death. All of a sudden she found herself telling him that the baby had died along with Noura. She'd been afraid to tell the truth: she was scared and didn't know what to do. She'd entrusted the baby to Adèle al-Naa'es, a European family had adopted him, and she'd spent the initial sum of money the woman had given her to open a kiosk. She had nothing left.

When Taymour learned that Noura and the child had died, he nearly fainted and then started crying. Sabah was taken aback by the sight of a grown man crying like a little boy. When she saw him like this, she left him and went to the kitchen to make him a glass of cold lemonade with orange blossom water.

In the kitchen Sabah started thinking about whether or not it was good that she'd hidden the truth. She wondered about how useful telling the truth would be, rationalizing to herself that she'd acted correctly, and that nothing good— only harm—could come from saying what was true.

Why say the truth? What's the use? I kept it hidden and I let her son live happily—how could he live here? A murdered mother, an imprisoned father ... Let him think that he is from a Dutch, Danish, or French family. God knows what country he's gone to. It's better like this for everyone.

Sabah dropped the glass of lemonade she'd been holding as she was putting it on a tray. She poured the rest of the lemonade in the glass pitcher into another cup for Taymour. Her mind was scattered, her hands trembling. None of these rationalizations, which she repeated to herself while squeezing the lemons and dissolving the sugar into the liquid, worked. An involuntary sound escaped her as she was collecting the pieces of shattered glass off the ground. *If Karim were still here, he would have told me, "Good morning Sabah," and I would have squeezed lemonade for him and put in a lot of sugar.* Then she started to cry.

She picked up the tray with the glass of cold lemonade on it and went back into the sitting room, presenting it to Taymour, who was leaning his body forward and resting his forehead in the palm of his hand. He'd lit a cigarette. His skin and face were blood red; he was smoking, and staring at the floor.

"I don't know why I lied at that moment," Sabah told Maya. "What pushed me to invent that story? Why did I tell him the child died? Why didn't I tell Taymour the truth?"

Sabah started repeating her questions, while hitting the sides of her head with her hands, rhythmically, as if they were at a Sufi religious ceremony. Sabah kept talking, but Maya was struck silent.

"I don't know what happened. I was afraid he would kill him, kill Karim, after I saw him in Noura's apartment when

I went there again. The place had been turned upside down like a bomb had exploded inside. Oh my God, if the child had been there what would he have done to him? He threatened me: 'Don't you dare come back here unless you want what happened to her to happen to you.' He laughed: 'I will kill you and put you in a car near an explosion.' He opened the apartment door and threw me outside. He pushed me down the stairs and I tumbled down like a ball. My back injury is from that day. I have never properly healed since then and I can't work like I could before. I was afraid to say anything. He might have eliminated me like he did her. I didn't dare go back to my place with Karim for six months.

**

Shawqi, the mukhabarat officer, searched Noura's flat for Henaa's letter and her new writings, perhaps other papers as well. Perhaps he'd found out that Noura had written more than the story she published, and he wanted to erase every-thing, every single thing, Maya thought. Maya asked Sabah for Adèle al-Naa'es's address or the name of someone else who knew her and could help. She replied that she didn't know. She told her that her friend Mariam had introduced her to Adèle. But Mariam died last year.

Sabah remained in her neighborhood and waited. Perhaps she was waiting for hope, perhaps an illusion. But she was like everyone else who hunkered down in place during the war and got used to it. She was neither an angel nor a devil, but both at the same time. To stay alive, they had to awaken the devil dormant inside them, entrust him with steering the wheel at the helm, and leave him freedom of choice. They trusted him because he alone let them stay alive, far from death, or far from the gods who collude with death.

Despite all this, Maya still asked herself every day why Sabah had lied.

Things happen that are difficult to explain easily. Sometimes we do things whose traces we carry around inside of us. These things put us within a frame quite different from any image that we might wish to see ourselves reflected in. But this is us: we feed the poor, we laugh at a passing joke, we love, we mourn, we dance, but we also kill our neighbors in civil wars. Since we are like that, how can we describe ourselves?

Maya got up to leave Sabah's flat, but before she opened the door, she turned to ask what Noura looked like—what color was her hair, what color were her eyes?

These questions stunned Sabah. But at the same time they also relaxed her, for they distracted her from the depressing atmosphere their conversation had conjured up.

She looked at Maya, then took a deep breath and wiped her tears with the sleeve of her shirt, before answering, "Like Asmahan...."

16
DECEMBER 1994

Maya finished working on the film. She wanted to celebrate with Danny at Sarah's café. Danny couldn't stay long because he had to meet Ernest, who was waiting for him in front of Beirut Theatre so they could go to a play together.

Sarah poured Maya a glass of red wine and asked, "What's after the film? Will you work here with me? I would need you only on the weekends. That way you would still have enough time for your writing."

"I don't know," Maya answered. "Give me a few weeks. I want to first finish my research into both Adèle al-Naa'es and the process for adopting a child. I want to know who this woman is and where he is as well."

"Have you called Kemal?" Sarah asked.

"Not yet," Maya replied. "I don't know what to tell him … or how."

Sabah said that she didn't know where Adèle al-Naa'es lived. All she had was the phone number of the obstetrician

Adèle had given her, but that no one answered. It seemed that the doctor was dead, his clinic closed. Maya searched everywhere for the name of this woman, but to no avail. She went to the archives of the *An-Nahar* and *As-Safir* newspapers. She searched in the local news for stories of children being sold during the war and found nothing. She turned up many stories about children who'd been left on the steps of orphanages, monasteries, and Islamic charities. But no mention of adoptions; and there is no such thing as adoption in Islam. Maya wasn't even sure if the Lebanese state had laws allowing adoption at all—regardless of the community or sect of the child and of the family seeking to adopt.

"I still can't believe that Sabah sold the baby," Sarah said.

"Is it really possible that all this happened in the total absence of any media coverage?" Maya asked. "Nothing about this woman, not even on the issue of selling babies. Is this possible? A child evaporates just like that, and no one even knows he's left Lebanon? And then doesn't an adoption need an obstetrician, a lawyer, a judge, or even a priest or some local authorities to permit the child to leave the country?"

"But don't forget the war!" Sarah replied. "Noura's son was taken out of Lebanon in 1978, and you know the situation people were living in at that time. You were following what was happening, even if you were in France."

Maya asked, "OK, so it was war, but what now? Do we just shut up and always stay silent because of the war?" During her research over the preceding two weeks, Maya found very few investigative articles in the local press of the time exposing the wartime networks that sold children. These articles were short, unclear, and didn't reveal the names of the gang members. But she had photocopied them. Sitting in the café, Maya and Sarah now read through them.

"Was Adèle al-Naa'es the gang leader?" Sarah wondered aloud while Maya was reading all the articles related to the subject, passing them on to her. Did she take advantage of Sabah? Perhaps Karim wasn't the first child she sold, extorting money from the adoptive family on the pretext of paying fees for the legal proceedings she would have to undertake before travelling abroad with the child.

Perhaps the gang didn't consist solely of Adèle and her husband, but also other people; perhaps they colluded with security services or illegal organizations to falsify the child's identity documents. Otherwise how did they let a tiny, breastfeeding infant leave Lebanon—through the airport, the port at Jounieh, or the land border at Masnaa—without even one of his parents?

"I'm going to call Kemal," Maya told Sarah. "I know he will come to Beirut at the end of the week, but I can't wait. I have to tell him what I found out."

On the phone, Maya told him about the last pages of Noura's diary, her meeting with Sabah, and what she'd read in the local papers.

"Kemal, it might not have been only Karim, but hundreds of other children, or even more. Forgetting isn't only just about forgetting the identities of the killers and the kidnappers, but also about forgetting the identities of those people who profited from the war—the ones who floated among the killers and kidnappers. The tragedy isn't that they're unknown but that no one wants to know. No one wants to remember. Those who died, died. Those who emigrated, emigrated. Those who remained here either invented a new fictional story or stayed silent. The story is lost among international flights, graveyards, and the state administration. These people are no place. Invented memories are absurdity, but people hold onto absurdity. They don't dare do otherwise. Without an invented memory, they discover that only emptiness resides within them."

Kemal remained silent, as if what Maya were telling him was a lot in one go. Karim was somewhere in this world. *He's alive!* So whispered his heart.

"Kemal …" Maya said, just to be sure he was still on the line.

A vision of Noura passed through Kemal's mind—her asleep on the beach, a shadow of the gentle roundness of her pregnancy emerging on her belly. He was still holding the phone.

"Oh Maya…. If you only knew," came his deep voice, sounding astonished. Then silence again.

"Kemal …" Maya repeated. She heard his rhythmic breathing. She kept the receiver pressed to her ear. He also was listening to her, thinking he could close his eyes and listen to her forever. He could surrender now to this warm voice coming from Beirut and fall asleep. He could turn the years backward to an earlier time, before he stopped hunting for happiness.

**

On her second visit to the newspaper archives, Maya found some issues from 1993 and 1994 that reported on young European women and men who came to Lebanon to search for their biological parents. Maya took the photocopies of everything she'd found in the local papers and sat in a café on Hamra Street.

One short article was about a young Danish man who came to Beirut to search for his parents, who, he said, were Lebanese. Another article concerned a Swedish woman's visit to Beirut. The articles didn't mention their ages. A photograph of the young man showed him to be in his twenties. But Kemal and Noura's son was now seventeen years old, Maya thought. Perhaps this young man was in fact seventeen, she reasoned, and the photo just made him seem a bit older. A third report was about a group of young people who came from Holland to search for their true identities. Maya looked at the picture of these young people, examining their faces and hair. Focusing in particular on one of the young men from Holland, she imagined that he was Karim. But in the one photograph she did have of the young Karim, he had thick, curly hair. "Hair changes, perhaps it's him," she told Sarah on the phone.

"This is madness!" Sarah said, adding, "You won't be able to recognize him; he left Lebanon at six months old, and you don't even have any other picture of him!"

Most of the young people returned to Europe after they lost hope of finding a thread or a light to guide them. They brought their identity papers, which their European parents had saved, showing that they were Lebanese. But as soon as they started searching through official circuits, they found out that these documents were forged by agencies in Lebanon and they wouldn't find any trace of their own names or the names of the people supposed to be their biological parents. An obstetrician's name was repeated in the articles. It was that of the same doctor Maya had tried in vain to call after Sabah gave her the number. The doctor died at the beginning of 1990. No doubt there were hundreds of children like them, Maya reasoned, children who left Lebanon illegally during the war.

**

Maya's cell phone rang. It was Sarah: "Come over, let's have lunch together before Shadi gets out of school." Maya left the café. It was raining. She put her handbag on her head and headed toward her car. She had wanted to write down a lot more.

It was the last month of the year, and the street was preparing for Christmas. The decorations were different than in previous years. Hamra Street was delightful despite the heavy rain. To Maya it seemed as if the war had not passed through here, as if it were, at most, a faded, even disappeared memory. Maya felt she could stay in Beirut and not leave again. Aida was attached to Shadi and didn't want them to go abroad. And then Sarah had offered her a good job, one that wouldn't take up too much time. Kemal flashed through her head like a bolt of lightening and warm feelings flooded her.

Maya stepped off the sidewalk to cross to the other side of the street, where she had parked her car. Just then three cars were careening by at an insane speed, and someone fired a gunshot out the open window of one of them. A warlord who'd become a MP and then became a government minister was racing by in his convoy. Shouts from the windows of the cars accompanying the motorcade ordered pedestrians—who for their part were hiding their faces from the rain with umbrellas—to clear the road. Frightened drivers stopped their cars on the side of the road to let the motorcade through. As Maya started to run, she tried to jump over a pothole filled with a little pool of rainwater. One of the cars in the motorcade crashed into her. Her small body flew through the air like a kite and landed on a pile of sandbags in front of a newly restored building. She felt a strong blow hit her limbs. A pain in her shoulder and leg. Grainy images passed in front of her, butterflies fell, their colors faded, their sounds sporadic. She looked around her as a hot liquid ran down her neck and face. She wanted to stand up, to move her body—but she couldn't. She didn't hear anything after that.

Later she was told that in the ambulance she asked only one question: "Is the airport open?" She mumbled that she wanted to leave with Shadi. She wanted to survive with him. Then she lost consciousness.

**

"I lost Noura and I don't want to lose you," Kemal told her the next afternoon when he visited her in the hospital. It was

Sarah who'd called him to report the accident.

Maya opened the little envelope that was attached to the bouquet of flowers Kemal had brought her. In it was a note that read, "Maya, when I saw you in front of the door of my hotel room, I hesitated for a long time. I was vaguely afraid—perhaps of a second loss, which I couldn't bear. The moment you entered, I felt that you were entering my life and wouldn't leave it."

She gazed at him. Her eyes looked like two birds peering out of a small window of her white prison of gauze wrapped around her head and neck, plaster casts covering her right arm and her two broken legs.

"I didn't mean to be a heroine, I'm one by chance," she told him with good-natured irony. He smiled and said, after a moment of silence, "I'll find Karim, Maya. We will find him."

In the evening, when she was lying on her hospital bed, Maya used her left hand to write the first sentence of her novel: "I didn't know that we would become the story that we haven't yet told."

Paris, Spring 2015

AFTERWORD

In the summer of 2015, scenes of Syrian refugees—particularly women and children—sitting on flimsy boats and dinghies crossing the Mediterranean Sea to flee fighting at home captured the world's attention. Watching these scenes from the relative comfort of Lebanon was, every day, a heartbreaking reminder of the human toll of civil war, and the countless lives forever affected—and ended—by fighting. In Lebanon at the same time, inspirational scenes of young people fighting against the corruption and cynicism of the ethically bankrupt sectarian system of government offered a counterbalance of hope that perhaps ordinary people could have some impact on the shape of their future. As people in Lebanon—young and old—took to the streets, Khandaq al-Ghamiq, the old Beirut neighborhood so prominent in this novel, was in the news. The proverbial "bad apples" singled out by the power structure to blame unrest upon, the "young thugs of Khandaq al-Ghamiq," were caricatured in the media in order to shift attention from

239

the very real demands of disenfranchised people in Lebanon seeking to hold the government accountable. These people were represented by a loose coalition of groups with such names as "We Want Accountability" and "You Stink."

The scenes from the summer of 2015 are crucial to my reflections here because we know that translations both directly and indirectly reflect their own times, circumstances, and contexts as much as those of the texts they are transforming. My translation of *The Weight of Paradise* was finished in an atmosphere that in many ways reflected the circumstances of its characters, though the story is set so many years earlier, between the 1970s and 1990s. Against the background of the present, working with a text about Syrian women fleeing to Lebanon only to be confronted by war, the devastation of the center of Beirut (where Khandaq al-Ghamiq is located), and its rehabitation by internally displaced refugees, the novel felt oddly prescient and deeply engaged in contemporary events.

This translation in some ways mirrors the journeys of its characters in moving across borders, from place to place, firmly rooted in the complicity of women. The novel itself was finished in Paris; the translation's first draft was completed in Montreal, and it was finished in Beirut. But in some ways, fittingly, the bulk of the work on the translation itself was a collaborative endeavor undertaken in the spacious, wind-filled rooms of an old house in the hills of Ain Anoub, a village overlooking Beirut—the house itself a symbol and remnant of the war.

In a recent interview I asked Iman Humaydan what was similar or different about the translation of this novel and other translations of her works. She gave an answer that I myself might have given: this translation is different because more than any previous translation that either one of us had been involved in, its final shape is a product of us working so closely together.

For over a month in the summer of 2015, Iman and I lived together in that house in Ain Anoub, not only working on the translation for a few hours a day but also sharing our space, time, and thoughts about both it and many other things. This means that the histories she had drawn upon in writing this novel were all powerfully present in the lived context in which the translation was finished. This proximity also meant that our discussions about everything from daily affairs to bigger questions were all a part of our creative process. My reflections on translating *The Weight of Paradise*, including choosing this new name for the novel, are all thus linked to this shared time and space.

The original title of this novel in Arabic more literally reads *50 Grams of Paradise*, alluding to the specific weight the Egyptian perfume seller attributes to his scent of the same name when he offers it to Kemal in the novel. Formal and informal conversations with people throughout the spring and summer demonstrated to me that this title did not have the same appealing resonance in English as it did in Arabic, and conjured up the well-known bestseller of the times, *50 Shades of Gray*, or invoked drug dealing rather than perfume. We experimented with many titles. I would suggest one and let it sit for a while; we would debate it, discuss it, leave it, and come back to it. No title felt right until *The Weight of*

Paradise emerged—words that capture the idea of weighing the perfume as well as the notion of paradise not always being where or what we expect it to be. Our close proximity and constant conversations allowed both of us to try out different word combinations in-between other tasks and to arrive at a compromise we both were satisfied with.

Another way in which our close collaboration helped the translation in the summer of 2015 was through our working together on ways to solidify the PEN Association of Lebanon, by discussing, writing, and translating materials for it. This association for the freedom of speech and expression is tied to the work of characters like both Noura and Maya, the novel's twin protagonists. Working together on the same kinds of issues as the book's characters once again tied our real-life collaboration to their fictional ones—the life of the Lebanese past to ours in the present.

What I hope *The Weight of Paradise* in English translation offers its readership is a journey through words and language to ponder the past. This book is about how we do and don't repeat history, how we can look at and understand history in different ways. It is about real-life people and their everyday lives, but in extraordinary times—like perhaps all times are. Iman Humaydan's latest novel offers a way to think about all of these things and about how people can and do live, love, and resist oppression in any time and in any place.

TRANSLATOR'S ACKNOWLEDGMENTS

This translation, more than any I have ever completed, was truly a collaborative effort, and the first and most profound thanks are due its author, with whom every word, phrase, section, and idea was reviewed, discussed, and debated in beautiful Ain Anoub, Lebanon. It is insufficient to say merely "thank you" to Iman Humaydan. As always the staff at Interlink Books was supportive and professional. A grateful acknowledgement is owed to Michel Moushabeck, Publisher at Interlink, and to copy editor Paul Olchváry, who worked carefully with me to clean up and polish the language of this book. A number of other people read and discussed parts of the translation with me and us, giving different kinds of support and feedback. I gratefully acknowledge Malek Abisaab, Rula Jurdi Abisaab, Katy Kalemkerian, Marcia Lynx Qualey, and Mira Younes. Thanks to Samira Aghacy and Miriam Sfeir for inviting me to present portions of this translation and my thoughts about it as work in progress at the Lebanese

American University. As all such intensive work demands the patience and support of the people who surround you, I would like here to acknowledge Yasmine Nachabe Taan, the rest of the Nachabe/Taan family, Aziz Choudry, and Tameem Hartman for both discussions and the space that allowed the work to get finished.

The Weight of Paradise is partly about friendship, particularly women's friendship, in different places and through displacements, and so I dedicate this translation therefore to someone who has known all of those with me, Yasmine.